I0716313

ALEX CAGE
CLEAN FAST-PACED ACTION THRILLERS

JOIN THE READER'S LIST

Get the latest releases and exclusive giveaways - sign up to the Alex Cage Reader List:

www.AlexCage.com/signup

ALSO BY ALEX CAGE

Zambaa Superhero Series

Zambaa: Mask and Gauntlets

Zambaa: Unchained

Orlando Black Series

Carolina Dance

Bayside Boom

Bet on Black

Leroy Silver Series

Contracts & Bullets

Aloha & Bullets

Politics Thieves & Bullets

Get the latest releases and exclusive giveaways, sign up to the Alex Cage Reader List.

www.AlexCage.com/signup

ZAMBAA: UNCHAINED

ALEX CAGE

CHAPTER ONE

THE LATE AFTERNOON sun shone bright in the downtown Chicago sky, but below on the crowded street in front of the courthouse, tensions were high. Facing the building stood a group of nearly thirty shouting protesters, waving signs in the air.

"He belongs behind bars!"

"Curtis Sharpe has most of Chicago in his pocket!"

"Don't let that scum off!"

Tripp Coleman stood front and center among the protesters. He wasn't holding a sign or shouting. His focus was on the courthouse's front doors, behind the line of police officers standing in front of him. Coleman had an athletic physique with an above average height and wore boots, jeans, a silver chain necklace, and a dark hoodie. With his head uncovered, his hood beat against his back as it flapped in the light, cool breeze.

An officer in full police riot gear approached where Coleman stood. "Get back," he said to the crowd.

The group continued to shout while the officer stared at them. He then glared at Coleman who was now only feet away. Coleman folded his arms and stared back. The officer looked him up and down before joining his coworkers back in line.

Coleman felt someone brush against his shoulder, and as he turned, he heard a familiar voice say, "Don't pay them no mind, Tripp. And don't sweat it—there's no way he's getting off."

Coleman glanced at a shorter, stocky guy to his right. The man had a low fade cut, the same as Coleman, and mocha brown skin, also the same as Coleman.

"What's up, Rod?" Coleman said, while moving his attention back to the courthouse.

"Just checking on you, man."

"I'm fine."

From his peripheral, Coleman saw Rod staring at him.

"What? I said I'm fine, Rodney."

Rodney kissed his teeth. "Man, you know I don't like my full name."

Coleman chuckled. "Yeah, I know."

At that, the front doors to the courthouse opened and two men toting a podium teetered outside. They rested the podium a few yards behind the line of police officers. One man placed a microphone in the podium's holder while the other sat a pair of speakers on the pavement on either side of the podium. The men then walked back inside the building. Shortly after, a woman dressed in a dark suit skirt exited the doors, followed by a man in a slate-blue suit. Tailing the blue suit was someone Coleman had seen before. The man wore a tailored black suit and had slicked-back, dark-brown hair. Other than his eyebrows, there was no facial hair over his fair skin. His name was Curtis Sharpe.

As Sharpe followed the man and woman to the podium, he looked out at the crowd with beady eyes and a smirk on his face. The woman tapped the microphone and a thump echoed from the speakers.

She smiled. "Can you hear me?" she asked over the crowd's commotion.

"Ain't nobody tryna hear you," Rodney said. "Representing a murderer."

Coleman said nothing. Just kept his arms folded and listened to her.

"I know you're all here for the verdict," she continued, before pointing to the man in the blue suit. "My colleague and I are happy to announce our client, Mr. Sharpe, is cleared of all allegations."

Coleman's eyes widened, and Rodney gasped as the chants from the crowd grew louder.

"We believe the justice system has spoken, and the right decision was made. Thank you," the woman said before stepping away from the podium. She placed a hand on Sharpe's shoulder and directed him toward a limo parked on a street perpendicular to the main road.

Colman felt heat rise from his gut and his throat drying as he glared at Sharpe.

"We'll get our own justice!" someone yelled from the crowd.

Suddenly, a small brick soared from the crowd. It shone crimson red as it crested an arch in the air, then descended toward the line of police officers. The brick smacked an officer's helmet and sent the man stumbling to the ground.

"Fire!" one officer yelled.

A loud pop filled the air and a small cylinder tube streaming a trail of smoke flew into the crowd of protesters. Many from the group shouted and charged toward the line of officers.

"Yo, Tripp, let's get outta here, man," Rodney said.

Coleman didn't respond. Just stared through the smoke and watched as Sharpe and his lawyers raced toward the limo.

"C'mon! Let's go!"

Coleman calmly threaded through the boisterous crowd toward the limo.

"Where're ya goin'?" Rodney continued as Coleman walked to a blockade, just yards away from the vehicle.

A bald, muscular man opened the limo's back door and guided Sharpe to it. Before entering, Sharpe looked over his shoulder at Coleman. The two locked eyes. With a sour look, Sharpe glanced Coleman up and down, then ducked inside the limo. Sharpe's lawyers attempted to enter the vehicle, but the muscular man shoved them away before ducking inside himself and immediately shutting the door. The limo sped off, leaving the lawyers to fend for themselves as they raced toward the courthouse's main entrance.

"C'mon, Tripp, let's go," Rodney said while pulling at Coleman's arm.

Coleman yanked his arm from Rodney's grip and continued to stare at the limo as the vehicle's tires screeched on a sharp turn.

"Get on the ground!" Coleman heard as a sting pierced his side.

He turned and saw a police officer brandishing a nightstick, with electrical probes at its tip glowing a lightning blue.

Coleman gritted his teeth and snatched the nightstick away from the officer before gripping the man's protective face mask and shoving him to the ground. Towering over the policeman, Coleman raised the nightstick. The officer hollered and used his arms to shield his face as Coleman glared at him and positioned the stick to strike. Another sting hit Coleman's back, then another on his side. He dropped the nightstick, and a swarm of officers encircled him.

"Tripp!" Rodney yelled as Coleman fell to the ground.

Coleman saw boots surrounding him, hands clawing at him, a nightstick coming at his face, then blackness.

CHAPTER TWO

EIGHTEEN HOURS LATER and four blocks away, Calvin Bush dashed along a busy sidewalk. Adjusting the backpack straps over his shoulders, he threaded around some passersby before stopping at a crosswalk. As cars honked, Bush rubbed his hand across his low, faded hair, then across his forehead, wiping beads of perspiration away. His phone rang.

"Hi, Norm," he answered.

"What's up, bud?" Norman said through the phone. "Didn't see you this morning, again."

"Yeah, I'm running late."

Running late had become a frequent occurrence for Bush since acquiring his abilities. He had stayed up late the night before, rescuing people from a burning building, then helping fire and rescue crews put out the fire.

"Yeah, getting used to that," Norman replied. "I'll just catch you around lunchtime."

The crosswalk light turned green.

"Okay. That sounds good. Gotta go."

As Bush crossed the street, sirens wailed behind him. On the main road to his left, four police squad cars raced past.

Bush's backpack moved, and he felt a poke to his back, followed by a voice saying, "We gonna check that out?"

Bush shook his head and sighed before veering into an empty alley. He ducked behind a dumpster, kneeled, and shrugged off his backpack. As he unzipped the backpack, voices flowed from inside it.

"Me first."

"You are the most rude, Baadaye."

"Shhh," Bush uttered with a finger to his lips.

A golden right-handed gauntlet hovered from the bag. Two amber stones shone on the back of the gauntlet. One stone sat between the index and middle knuckles, and the other between the ring and pinky knuckles. A large, purple stone sat center on the backhand of the gauntlet and glowed as the words, "Don't shush me," were said. "You've been keeping us in that prison for months."

"Chill out, Baadaye. You're being dramatic," Bush said.

"That appears to be his nature," a voice said as an identical looking left-handed gauntlet floated from the bag. "Rude and dramatic."

Baadaye pointed his thumb to the other gauntlet. "Leave it to Zamani to psychoanalyze," he said. "Because he's such a *people's person*," Baadaye continued, using his index and middle fingers to create air quotes on people's person.

"Well, I have been known—" Zamani started.

"Guys," Bush interrupted. "We have a situation on our hands."

"You're right, Calvin. Let's get on with it."

"Let's do it," Baadaye followed up.

Bush stood with his arms raised to his sides while Zamani hovered to his left hand and Baadaye to his right.

"This part is so fun," Baadaye said as he and Zamani phased around Bush's hands and a bright golden flare covered Bush's entire body.

The gauntlets glowed, and Bush felt an electric sensation

flow throughout his body. Calf-high boots covered his legs, and a tight, durable spandex dressed his lower body. His upper body had the same material, but with distinct, golden African designs over it. A gold cloth wrapped around his waist, and a hooded cloak of the same color covered his head and draped to his ankles. Bush touched his face and felt a cloth mask around his eyes.

"Why do you always touch your mask?" Baadaye asked.

"I like to know my identity is protected," Bush said, his voice deeper.

"Your mask always appears. I think you're trying to make some kinda fashion statement."

"Worry not, Calvin," Zamani said. "We'll inform you if your identity is in jeopardy."

"I appreciate it," Bush said, while looking up at the sky. "Now, can we get to the situation at hand?" He bent his knees and his cloak glowed before he shot into the air. He cleared the alley's building and flew toward the police caravan.

"I wonder what the disturbance is," Zamani said.

"That makes two of us," Bush said as he descended toward the group of speeding vehicles.

The police raced after a black cargo van with a sunroof. The van threaded through traffic before reaching an open section of the street. As the police drew closer to the cargo van, the vehicle's sunroof slid open, and a gigantic cannon with an operator seat rose through the roof. The man operating the cannon wore full body armor and a helmet with a dark visor. He aimed the cannon at the police cars and the weapon droned before firing multiple rounds.

The squad cars leading the chase veered from the bullets' trajectory and crashed into vehicles parked at the curbs. Other police cars swerved and stopped in the middle of the street.

"Whoa!" Baadaye said.

"Oh my," Zamani uttered at the same time.

Bush grunted, then flew toward the cargo van. The man

behind the cannon swung his aim at him and fired. Bush used his arms to shield his head as a golden aura glowed around him and the bullets ricocheted off his body.

"He must not know about us," Baadaye said.

"That stings a little," Bush said before zooming to the van and landing on its roof in front of the cannon.

The cannon operator winced at Bush then toggled the cannon's joysticks. Bush shook his head as he grabbed the cannon's barrel with one hand and ripped it from the rest of the mechanism. The man jumped from the cannon's seat and steadied himself on the roof. Standing, he unholstered a pistol from his side and aimed it at Bush.

Bush stared at him while contorting his lips. "Man, c'mon. Really?"

"Not the brightest bulb in the store," Baadaye said.

The man fired four rounds. Bullets hit Bush's chest and dropped to the roof. The man's eyes widened behind the visors and his mouth gaped.

"Oh, that's more surprising than the cannon rounds bouncing off of us?" Baadaye continued.

Bush shook his head before raising his free hand at the man. Golden energy bands shot from Bush's hand and wrapped around the man's upper body, restraining his arms to his sides. As Bush walked toward the front of the van, he dropped the cannon's barrel, then flicked his hand and sent the man flying off the van. The guy's back struck a light pole while another golden band restrained him to the pole.

"Some must learn the hard way," Zamani commented.

Bush floated to the front of the vehicle. He stood on the hood and looked down at the windshield with folded arms. Inside, a man sat behind the wheel and another in the passenger seat. Both were in full tactical gear, identical to their partner from the cannon.

"Pull over, now," Bush said.

The two men stared at him for a moment with bulging

eyes before the man riding shotgun lifted a pistol at the windshield.

Bush cocked his head to the side. "Aight," he uttered before quickly hovering above the van.

He soared toward the back, grabbed the bumper with both hands, then lifted the vehicle off the street. The van's tires continued to spin as Bush carried the vehicle twenty feet into the air. He flew to an empty field near a small park and turned the van, so the driver's side hovered a few feet above the ground. Bush shook the vehicle. The driver's side door opened, and the men hollered as they dropped from the vehicle.

Bush descended toward the ground and rested the van on the grass next to the men. Standing, one man reached for the gun on his hip. Before the man could grab the gun, Bush shot an energy band at him. It tied the man's upper body and he dropped to the ground. Seeing the other guy sitting on his heels, Bush did the same to him before he could stand. The man fell to his side and groaned as he smacked the ground.

Bush walked toward the man. "You guys were packing some heavy firepower," he said. "Mind sharing what you were doing?"

The man scoffed and shook his head but said nothing.

"Of course you don't."

The squad cars approached the park, and Bush pivoted away from the restrained man. An officer emerged from one car and walked toward Bush.

"Thank you, Zambaa," the clean-shaved officer said. "These guys just robbed the Big Shoulders Central Bank, moments after it opened."

Bush glanced at the van. "A lot of firepower for a bank robbery."

The officer shrugged. "Yeah, if it wasn't for you, we probably would've never caught them."

Bush nodded. "Well, they're all yours," he said before walking a safe distance away, and then jetting into the sky.

It took Bush five minutes to get back to the alley, transform to regular Calvin, and make it to his office building. He zipped across the lobby to the elevators and took one to the seventh floor. Double doors with a plaque next to it which read, We Nail It, met him on the opposite side of the hall. Bush opened the doors and entered an office space. The sound of fingers striking keyboards and telephone conversations filled the air. As Bush walked to his cubicle, the aroma of coffee, egg, and sausage hit his nose. His stomach growled as he shrugged off his backpack and sat it on his desk.

"I forgot to grab something to eat," he uttered, staring at the opposite side of the floor.

Plastic sheeting, boxes, buckets, and tools littered that side of the office. Bush's thoughts went back to the fight which led to the renovations. As Zambaa, he had battled a powerful magic wielder. Bush and the man destroyed half the floor, beating on each other. That fight happened months ago, but nothing since had challenged Bush's powers like it. Taking down gangsters, extinguishing building fires, saving a malfunctioning plane, and catching bank robbers were all simple tasks for Zambaa.

Bush smiled at the thought before sitting at his desk.

"Calvin," a voice behind him called.

Bush glanced over his shoulder and saw a skinny, pale man with smooth skin and salt-and-pepper hair. He was George Rivers Junior, the CEO of the company, his boss, and typically a pain in the backside, but he had since mellowed after half of the office space was demolished.

Bush turned on his computer. "What's up, George?" he answered, facing the computer screen.

"When you get settled, can you swing by my office? I'm thinking about changing our purchase order software and would like your feedback."

Bush turned in his chair to face Mr. Rivers. "Okay," he said, nodding.

"Great. And Calvin?"

"Yeah?"

"Great work closing those invoices last week. It brought in a lot of money for us."

"Of course."

As Mr. Rivers left the cubicle, Bush felt his phone vibrate inside his pocket. He had a missed text message from Lisa.

How about dinner tonight?

Bush and Lisa grew up together as good friends. Over the past few months, a romantic interest blossomed between them, and they went on a few dates.

That sounds great, Bush texted.

Typing bubbles bounced at the bottom of the messaging screen, then came Lisa's reply. *I know I had to cancel our last date, and you had to take a rain check on our date before that, but I'm eager to make up for what we missed.*

Bush remembered the night he had to cancel. He didn't want to, but a news helicopter was in trouble. The aircraft hovered too close to a building crane and clipped it. Bush caught the helicopter before it crashed into the crowded streets. And the night Lisa canceled, Bush felt relieved, because he had to help clear an accident involving an 18-wheeler on the Skyway Bridge during the time of their scheduled date.

Me too.

Great! See you tonight.

Bush gave Lisa's message the thumbs up emoji before placing his phone back inside his pocket.

"I bet that's Lisa he's texting," Baadaye whispered from Bush's backpack.

"Indeed, it is," Zamani said.

"Shhh—you two," Bush said, placing the backpack onto the floor and sliding it under his desk.

"Lisa and Calvin sitting in a tree—" Baadaye sang in a low tone.

"Quiet," Bush nudged the backpack with his foot.

"Ouch. Okay."

Bush smiled, then turned to his computer and leaned back in his chair with his hands joined behind his head.

CHAPTER THREE

TWELVE BLOCKS AWAY, Tripp Coleman sat alone in a six-by-eight jail cell—his ribs bruised, his right eye sore, and his head aching. He looked toward the bars as footsteps approached. A chubby officer stopped at the door and unclipped a key ring from his belt. The keys on the ring jingled as he inserted one into the door.

"Someone's here to see you," the officer said, fiddling with the door.

Coleman squinted.

The officer pulled the door open. "Let's go."

Coleman glared at the man for a moment before standing and walking toward the door. He glanced the officer over as he exited the cell.

The chubby man closed the door, then pointed down the hall. "This way."

They walked toward the front of the station, but before they reached the busy lobby area, the officer directed Coleman to a door on the left.

"In there," the officer said.

Coleman stared at the officer before rolling his eyes and opening the door. He entered a small conference room with a rectangular table at the center. A woman sat at the opposite end of the table. She had alluring brown eyes, smooth almond skin, and a beautiful smile between heart-shaped lips. Coleman stood and looked at her, his mouth slightly gaped.

With her index finger, the woman brushed a strand of her short, natural curly hair from her face to behind her ear. "Don't worry—I'm here to help. Please, take a seat."

The door shut behind Coleman. He glanced at the door, then walked toward the table. As he approached, the woman stood and adjusted her suit skirt before extending a hand.

"Tiffany Stephens," she said.

Coleman shook her hand and nodded.

"Tripp Coleman, right?" she continued, still holding his hand.

Coleman nodded as they released each other's hand.

Tiffany fixed on his face. "What did they do to you?"

Coleman shrugged at the question. "Minor bruises. I'll be okay," he said, sitting in the chair opposite her.

"Yeah, but it shouldn't've happened," Tiffany said as she sat.

"Like I told the cops, I was just standing there before they attacked me."

"You didn't push an officer?"

"After he attacked me. Who are you?"

"I'm sorry. Gave you my name but forgot to mention I'm your attorney."

Coleman winced. "I don't have a lawyer."

"It's pro bono. I kinda moonlight for a civil-rights activist group. Your friend Rodney informed the group of your situation."

Coleman shrugged. "So, you can help get me outta here?"

"Absolutely. But can you answer a question for me?"

"Yeah."

"Why were you at Curtis Sharpe's ruling?"

Coleman glanced away but said nothing.

"Did someone you know receive treatment from Sharpe Medical Technologies?"

Coleman looked at Tiffany, then fixed on the table.

Tiffany sighed. "I only ask because we're building a case against him."

Coleman shrugged. "He's cleared of all charges," he said, shaking his head.

"Not all. We have other char—"

"You said you can help get me out."

Tiffany stared at Coleman while inhaling, before pursing her lips and slowly exhaling. She reached down to her brief-case and removed a cell phone.

"You're free to go," she said, pressing at her phone's screen. "Typical case of the police getting intimidated by an athletic, tall, good-looking black man." Tiffany closed her eyes and scoffed as if she wished she could take back what she said. Coleman smiled. She noticed and smiled back.

"So, I'm free to go? What changed their minds?"

"This," Tiffany said, turning her cell phone toward Coleman.

A video played. It showed Coleman standing outside of the courthouse among a rowdy crowd. He was looking toward Sharpe's limo. A moment later, an officer came into the frame and poked Coleman with a nightstick.

Tiffany turned the phone back to herself and tapped at the screen. "You were unjustly assaulted. They didn't know someone caught it on video. When I showed them this, they couldn't say much. Now the question I have for you is— would you like to pursue charges against the officers and the police department?"

Coleman thought back to the incident. Heat rose from his gut to his throat. He bit his bottom lip to conceal his rage. "No," he said.

Tiffany winced. "Are you sure?"

"Yeah," Coleman said with a sigh.

"I urge you to reconsider. They should be held accountable."

"They will," Coleman said in a firm tone.

Tiffany's eyebrows rose and her mouth gaped, but she said nothing. She glanced at the table before looking at Coleman. "Going through the proper legal channels is the best way."

"Like it was for Sharpe?"

Tiffany exhaled. "His time is coming."

Coleman stood. "I agree. Anything else? I'd like to get back some of the time I lost."

"Here's my card," Tiffany said as she stood and extended a business card to him.

Coleman took the card. "Thanks," he said before pivoting toward the door.

"Call me if you need anything," Tiffany said, as he exited the room.

"This way," the chubby officer said when Coleman entered the hall.

The officer led him to the lobby, and they threaded through a small crowd to a counter with a thick transaction window. A female officer, on the opposite side of the window, slid a clipboard under the glass. Coleman signed his name on the release form attached to the clipboard and slid it back. The woman slid him a bag with his keys, silver chain, and wallet. Coleman kissed the chain, then clipped it around his neck before placing his keys and wallet inside his pockets and walking toward the front entrance.

"Hope you enjoyed your stay with us," the chubby officer said before letting out a chuckle.

Without turning around, Coleman balled his fist and continued to the entrance. As he exited and landed on the sidewalk, he covered his eyes as they adjusted to the after-noon sun's glaring reflection from the surrounding buildings. Coleman heard footsteps approach him.

Rodney stepped next to him with his eyes and mouth wide open. "Oh man. They jacked you up. Black eye—and that knot on yo fo'head."

Coleman pulled his hoodie over his head. "Shut up. I don't need you reminding me. What you doing here?"

"I knew they were sending you a lawyer, so I wanted to check on you."

"Well, I'm out."

Rodney looked at Coleman's face before sucking in his lips and glancing at the ground. "Man. For real tho, I'm sorry," he said, shaking his head. "I'm really sorry, bro," he continued, his voice cracking.

Coleman slapped his friend's shoulder. "None of that—I'll be fine. Thanks for getting me the lawyer. She's good."

"Wait, they sent you a female lawyer?"

"Yep."

"How she look?"

Coleman smiled. "Pretty good."

Rodney squinted. "Did she have all the curves in the right places? Like I like?"

Coleman chuckled and shook his head as he walked up the sidewalk, dodging a few passersby on his way to the corner. Rodney followed him.

"So, you just gonna ignore my question?" he asked.

"Yep."

Cars honked and zoomed past as they stood with a crowd at the pedestrian's crossing.

"Did they feed you?" Rodney asked.

Coleman shook his head.

"Let's grab some lunch, then."

They walked for another seven minutes before arriving at a popular pizza spot. The place was clearing out as they entered. Coleman and Rodney both ordered a personal pan, deep dish, pepperoni pizza. They sat across from each other, and when they were halfway through their meals, Rodney looked up at the television.

"Oh, there's that super dude, Zaybae," he said.

Coleman glanced over his shoulder. On the television screen, he saw who he knew as Zambaa lifting a cargo van. Coleman shrugged and turned to his food.

"He caught some bank robbers."

"Yeah, so?" Coleman said before biting into a slice of pizza.

"You don't think it's cool we have a real-life superhero? A black superhero at that. Look at the sky, it's a bird, no it's a plane, no it's a brotha saving the day."

Coleman shook his head. "If you ask me, he's just a pet for this legal system. That doesn't help our problems," he said in between chews. "Ouch." He touched his jaw.

"Did the cops have anyone check you out?"

Coleman looked at Rodney, cocked his head to the side, and contorted his lips.

"Well, maybe you should go to the hospital and get checked out."

"Nah, I'm good. But see, these are the type of problems yo hero can't help us with. He'll have to disrupt the status quo."

"Don't worry, man. Sharpe will get his."

"Yeah, he will. What are your plans tonight?"

Rodney squinted and shrugged. "I don't have none," he said, shaking his head.

"Good. I wanna pay a visit to Sharpe's research facility."

CHAPTER FOUR

AFTER WORK, BUSH took the stairs to the lobby. He wanted to avoid the congestion at the elevators, so he could get home in time to prepare for his date with Lisa. It had been on his mind all day, and the big smile on his face showed it. As he approached the front entrance, he heard a familiar voice from behind.

"Missed you at lunch today, bud."

Bush turned to find a medium-sized man wearing a dark-gray suit. The clean-shaved guy had sandy-beige skin and undercut brown hair.

"What's up, Norm? Sorry about that. Came in late, so I worked through lunch."

Norman smiled wryly. "Likely excuse. I haven't been seeing much of you lately. I miss hanging out."

Bush shrugged. "I know, man. Just been so busy."

"Uh-huh."

"What?" Bush said while continuing toward the front door with Norman tailing him.

"I know what you've been doing."

Bush stopped walking. His heart skipped a beat. He

hadn't told anyone about his powers. Not Lisa, not Norman, not anyone. Bush squinted. "Whattaya mean?"

"I mean, you and Lisa been spending a whole lot of time together."

"Mind ya business, Norm," Bush said as he continued toward the automatic sliding doors.

Norman followed. "Where's she at, anyway?"

Bush smiled. "I'm sure she went straight home. We have dinner plans tonight."

Norman pointed at him. "See, that's what I'm talking about."

Bush laughed.

They passed through the door and stepped onto a busy sidewalk. Cars on the street honked and revved, and exhaust mixed with the aroma of street food filled the air. They followed a line of people to a bus stop at the corner.

"I'll catch you later, bud," Norman said, stopping near a pizza truck parked at the curb. He pointed at the truck. "Imma grab a bite. Had a small lunch."

Bush waved. "Alright. See ya tomorrow," he said before turning back to the line.

The line was barely moving. Bush looked at his watch, then his eyebrows rose, and he smiled as a thought came to him. He slid out of the line and circled the crowd before crossing the street. He walked two more blocks before darting into an empty alley. A stale odor struck his nose as he ducked behind a large recycling bin.

"C'mon out, you two," he said, unzipping his backpack.

Zamani floated from the backpack. "You're not taking the bus today?"

Baadaye whizzed out a second after. "We need to talk about alternative modes of transportation."

Bush grinned. "Exactly."

"I mean for us—not you."

"Let's go. I have a date with Lisa tonight."

"Splendid," Zamani said.

"Yay, great," Baadaye said with a sarcastic tone.

Zamani and Baadaye hovered to Bush. He closed his eyes as the gauntlets fused with his hands. A second later he opened his eyes as Zambaa and rocketed toward the sky. A golden streak followed him as he cleared a skyscraper and soared east. The people below looked like ants, and the vehicles like Micro Machines. The wind whistled and blew upon his face as he picked up speed. Twenty-five seconds later, he approached the roof of his apartment building. Bush slowed before gently landing on the rooftop and crouching behind a large HVAC unit. He scanned the area to make sure no one was around, then transformed into his normal self.

"There's nothing like an early evening flight," Zamani commented.

"Yeah, we hafta do that mo often," Baadaye followed up.

"Quiet, you two," Bush whispered while guiding the gauntlets into his backpack.

"There's no one around," Baadaye protested on his way inside.

Bush zipped the backpack, placed it over his shoulders, then headed down the fire escape. When he arrived at his unit, he unlocked the window's gate before lifting the window open and climbing into his bedroom. The room was spacious, but only contained a queen-sized bed and a long, thin dresser. Bush closed the gate and shut the window before pulling the window's curtain across and laying his backpack on the bed. As he unzipped the backpack, he heard Baadaye say, "We need to talk."

"About what?" Bush asked.

Baadaye darted from the backpack. "We're tired of being lugged around in that dark, hot—prison."

Bush smiled and shrugged while walking to the room's door. "Hot? You're from Africa. Plus, you don't hear Zamani complaining."

"Well, it can get rather cramped," Zamani said.

Bush walked into the living room with the two gauntlets hovering behind him. The open room flowed into a kitchen on his right and a dining area on the opposite end. Bush made a left into a small hallway.

"What do you mean, I'm from Africa?" Baadaye asked. "So were your ancestors."

"Here we go again," Bush said as he nudged open a door at the end of the hall.

"Yep. Here we go."

"Oh my," Zamani said, floating toward the opposite end of the hall. "I'll be in the living room, you two."

"Look," Bush said to Baadaye. "I'm going to the bathroom. Do you want to follow me in?"

"No. You kidding me? I'm a magical gauntlet, remember?"

"Meaning?"

"Meaning I can smell. And the last time I went into the bathroom after you, I almost passed out."

Bush rolled his eyes, then stepped into the bathroom and shut the door on the levitating gauntlet.

"We're going to finish this when you're done," Baadaye said from the opposite side of the door.

Bush shook his head and chuckled, thinking back to when he first met Zamani and Baadaye at the museum. When Baadaye first spoke, it nearly scared him to death, but now hearing the gauntlet's voice was more annoying than anything else. His mind then wandered to when Zamani and Baadaye first fitted with him. The power felt both scary and amazing.

Bush sighed. "How things have changed," he muttered.

After showering, putting on lotion and deodorant, and brushing his teeth, Bush wrapped a towel around his waist and exited the bathroom. He made it to the end of the hall before Baadaye zipped in front of him.

"We need to finish our conversation," the right-handed gauntlet said with his index finger pointed at Bush.

Bush scoffed. "Look, not right now. I have to get ready for my date," he said, scanning the living area and seeing Zamani at the dining room table flipping through a book. "Why can't you just go read a book like Zamani?"

"Really?"

Bush sighed and stepped around Baadaye on the way to his bedroom.

Baadaye floated behind him. "You're the one who should be reading."

"What?"

"Your Africa comment."

"You're still on that?" Bush said as he entered the bedroom.

"Yes, I am."

"You're homesick. I get it."

Baadaye wagged his index finger horizontally. "It's more than that. I've been around for centuries and have seen many nations come and go. Africa is full of love and richness. You should be more proud of it."

Bush looked at Baadaye while cocking his head to the side and exhaling. "I told you, I wanna go visit." Bush nodded then added, "We'll go when I have some time."

"But not just you," Baadaye continued. "Most African descendants here don't have any interest in Africa."

Bushed chuckled. "Are you okay?"

"Yea—yeah. I still don't like being stuffed in that backpack." Baadaye floated toward the door with his fingers curled. "But we can talk about that after you finish getting ready."

On his way out of the room, Baadaye passed Zamani.

"He presents a compelling argument," Zamani said.

Bush scoffed as he shrugged into a t-shirt. "Of course you'd take his side."

"Not taking sides. But I concur with his assessment of the African descendants here."

"Well, I don't think there's much I can do about that."

"Maybe you can do more than you think."

Bush peeked through the doorway and saw Baadaye hover into the living room. "I think he's homesick."

"That may be so, but it could be more."

Bush's eyebrows furrowed. "Like what?"

"Remember, Baadaye sees things we don't."

Bush winced, then his eyes and mouth widened. "Oh right. You mean he may be seeing something in the future? But I thought you two automatically shared what you see."

"It's true I get glimpses of the past and Baadaye of the future, but we don't have to share with each other."

"Why wouldn't he share?" Bush stepped toward the door. "If something's going on, we need—"

Zamani's fingers straightened, and his palm pressed toward Bush. "I will have a talk with him, so don't you worry," he said. "Finish preparing for your date."

The room's door glowed a golden tint, then closed as Zamani exited the room. Bush stared at the door for a moment before jolting his head, then stepping into a pair of slacks. He spent the next twenty minutes walking back and forth from his bedroom to the bathroom, dressing and freshening up. When he was done, he walked into the living room where Zamani and Baadaye were.

"Looking sharp," Baadaye commented.

"Chic, indeed," Zamani followed up.

Bush smiled and nodded. "Thanks guys."

Baadaye floated to Bush, and with his index finger and thumb, adjusted the collar of Bush's long-sleeve, button-down shirt.

"Playa," Baadaye said.

Bush chuckled. "How are you feeling? You okay?"

"Yeah. I'm okay. I talked to Zamani—"

Bush's eyes widened. "Oh, really?"

"Yep, and we have an idea."

"Idea?"

Zamani hovered to Bush's left shoulder. "Yes. It's an alternate way to transport us," he said.

"Really?"

"Really. Let us demonstrate."

Baadaye swooped to Bush's right hand, and Zamani to his left.

"Excited to see how this goes," Baadaye said.

"Wait. This's safe, right?" Bush asked.

"Absolutely," Zamani said.

The two gauntlets sparked a bright golden hue. Bush squinted and felt warmth as the glimmering lights grazed his hands. The gauntlets' brightness intensified. Bush closed his eyes, but beams of light penetrated his eyelids, so he turned his face away. Moments later, the intensity of the bright glow dampened. Bush looked at his hands and saw beaded bracelets. The bracelet's beads were gold, except for three. One bead was purple, with two amber-colored beads on either side of it.

"Whoa!" Bush said.

"Yep. Beats a hot, musty bag," came a familiar voice inside Bush's head.

"Baadaye?"

"Who else would it be?"

"Nah—it's just—different."

"Indeed," Zamani's voice entered Bush's mind. "We can speak through your thoughts. What do you think?"

"I don't know. You're the one in my head, you tell me."

"Smart Aleck," Baadaye said. "We can talk to you, but it doesn't mean we can read your mind."

"I like the beaded bracelets, but to be honest, I don't wanna hear you guys in my head all day."

"There's a simple solution," Zamani said.

"Hey, don't tell him," Baadaye protested.

"The purple bead on each bracelet acts as a dial. Just turn it until you hear it click."

"Why would you tell him that? What if we need to say something and he has us muted?"

As Baadaye talked, Bush rotated the purple bead on his right bracelet. He heard a click as Baadaye's voice disappeared.

Bush's eyebrows rose, and he smirked. "I like this," he said with a slight chuckle.

"I figured you would fancy that, for privacy and all."

"Yes. And you know how Baadaye can get sometimes." Bush turned the dial of his bracelet back on.

"I heard that," Baadaye said.

"Hmm. So, you guys can still hear, but I just won't be able to hear you."

"Yep. Now that you've seen it, I say we turn back."

"Unh-uh. I have to get to the restaurant, so you might as well stay like you are."

Bush grabbed his cellphone, wallet, and keys, then exited the apartment. Not wanting to wrinkle or dishevel his clothes by flying, he hailed a cab. The ride to the restaurant took fourteen minutes, a few minutes longer than usual because of traffic. They parked near the curb, and Bush paid the driver then exited under the night sky and onto a foot-traffic-heavy sidewalk. He dodged around a crowd and a few passersby before arriving at an establishment with the words Mastro's Grille written above the door.

"Elegant," Zamani commented.

"Looks expensive," Baadaye followed up.

"Guys," Bush whispered.

"Just saying."

Bush walked inside, where a host greeted him and asked about his reservation. The host informed him that Lisa hadn't yet arrived, so Bush stepped back outside to wait. It wasn't long before she arrived in a taxi. As she exited the vehicle's back seat, Bush goggled at the sight. She wore a black halter dress, and her hair sat in a high puff. Bush fixed on her caramel brown face as she smiled, and her dimples cut into her high cheeks.

"You can pick your tongue off the ground," Baadaye said to Bush as Lisa approached.

"Shut up," Bush mumbled.

"Well, don't you look handsome," Lisa said.

"You—you look absolutely amazing."

Lisa batted her eyes and smiled. "Thank you."

Bush continued to stare with his mouth gaped.

"Perhaps you should escort the lady into the restaurant," Zamani said.

"And keep your mouth closed. It's embarrassing," Baadaye said.

"Quiet," Bush grumbled.

"What?" Lisa asked.

"You ready to eat?"

"Yes."

"Let's go," Bush said, guiding her to the entrance.

As Bush and Lisa entered the restaurant, he clicked the dials off on both bracelets.

CHAPTER FIVE

FOUR BLOCKS AWAY, Coleman and Rodney stood across the street from a fenced-in, two-story building. The structure sat close to some abandoned warehouses in a somewhat desolate area.

"I need to get in there," Coleman said.

"Fa real?" Rodney asked.

Coleman looked at him.

Rodney scoffed and shook his head. "This whole time I thought you were just venting. Didn't think you'd actually go through with it. You just got outta jail, and I'm not tryna go in."

"That's why I said I'm going in. Just need you to distract the guard. I've been watching this place for some time. They only have one guard outside tonight, so it should be easy." Coleman lifted a crowbar.

Rodney winced at the sight. "Wait, you've been—you know what—never mind." He sighed. "What about the inside?"

"Don't think they have more than two guards inside tonight. This is the day they have a shipment, and I've only ever seen one guard come out the building to help the driver who's always alone."

"Whatta ya think they shipping?"

"I'll find out when I'm inside."

"You're seriously gonna go through with this? Nothing I can say to talk you out of it?"

Coleman slowly inhaled, then exhaled and shook his head.

"Oh boy. What's the plan?"

Coleman half-smiled, then explained his plan to Rodney.

Seven minutes later, Coleman stood near the east corner of the facility with his crowbar in hand. He watched as Rodney lobbed rocks toward the west end of the building. One struck a fence pole, and the thump echoed all the way to Coleman. When the guard turned his attention toward the noise and walked in that direction, Coleman pulled his hood over his head, kneeled at the fence, then placed his crowbar on the ground while removing a pair of wire cutters. He snipped a vertical slit between the chain links and pried it open. He glanced in the guard's direction before putting away the cutters. When he saw it was clear, he grabbed his crowbar, kissed his necklace, then crawled through.

Once on the opposite side, Coleman raced to the building and pressed his back against the wall. He peeked around the corner and saw the guard's silhouette standing near the far west corner. Coleman ducked back behind the wall. Directly above him hung a camera, and to his right, a door with a card reader. With his back still against the wall and his eye on the camera, he inched toward the door. It was locked. He expected that much. Coleman thrust the crowbar's chisel edge between the door's jamb and metal locking mechanism, then pushed against the crowbar. The door popped open, and the lock components clinked.

Coleman wasted no time entering the building. He stepped

into a dimly lit hallway with two doors along each wall. At the opposite end was a commercial steel double door. Coleman walked down the hall, checking the doors on each side as he did. Only one room had furniture, a desk and a chair. The other rooms were completely empty. When Coleman reached the steel door, he turned the knob and discovered to his surprise that it was unlocked. On the other side, a large warehouse space greeted him. Crates, bins, and barrels sat scattered on the floor. A few doors lined the perimeter walls. Coleman stepped toward a door on his right, but stopped when he heard footsteps approach. He quickly ducked behind a crate. As the footsteps drew closer, Coleman's heart rate increased.

The footsteps stopped, and Coleman clutched his crowbar. He could feel the person near him. After a few seconds, the footsteps continued, but in the opposite direction. Coleman peeked over the crate and saw a guard walking toward the far end wall. Coleman noticed a door to his left and figured he'd start searching there first. He caught a whiff of an unusual odor as he dodged around some barrels with *Flammable* written on them in a bold red.

Upon entering the room, Coleman immediately noticed a workbench across the room from him. Flask, test tubes, beakers, and canisters littered the bench top. As Coleman walked to the bench for a closer look, a glow from the back of the room caught his eye. Situated against the back wall was another workbench with a computer station on top. Coleman walked to the bench and saw a paused video on the computer screen. The still frame displayed a smiling man with his hand in front of his face. The hand looked metallic. Curious about the video, Coleman reached for the computer's mouse, but a three-ring binder near the computer's keyboard caught his eye. He opened the binder. The first page had CSHP1M3T written bold and centered.

"CSHP1M3T," Coleman said to himself.

He flipped through the binder and landed on a page with

a lot of letters, circles, lines, and hexagons. It reminded him of something he saw years back in his high school chemistry class. As Coleman continued turning the pages, he heard footsteps behind him. He pivoted with his crowbar raised.

"Hey man—it—it's me," Rodney said, shrinking back with his arms raised.

Coleman winced. "Rodney?" He exhaled and lowered the crowbar. "Man, whatchu think you doin?"

"I'm ya boy. I gotta have ya back."

"You almost had the back of this crowbar. How'd you get in here?"

Rodney shrugged. "The same way you did." He nodded at the binder. "You find sumpin'?"

Coleman hunched his shoulders. "Not sure," he said, shaking his head and turning back to the binder.

He flipped through a few more pages and saw a picture of the same man on the computer screen. But in the picture, the man looked frail and out of breath.

Coleman shared his gaze between the binder and the screen. "Same dude," he muttered.

"What?" Rodney asked.

Coleman raised a finger, requesting a bout of silence. He grabbed the mouse and clicked the play button on the video, and the man on the screen began waving his metallic hand.

The results are astounding, came a deep male voice through the speakers as the video rolled. *CSHP1M3T will change millions of lives.* Coleman lowered the volume as the video transitioned to a clear canister with a translucent, reddish-brown liquid inside of it. *The compound works with the natural metals in the human body to regenerate damaged tissue.* The video continued to an outline of a human body with a severed left leg. *With a simple procedure, any human limb can be restored.* The video showed a needle labeled CSHP1M3T entering the human silhouette, then the missing limb grew into a leg matching the opposite side.

Rodney placed his hand over his mouth, and his eyes widened. "Man. That's some wild stuff."

Coleman rewound the video to the man with the metallic hand and paused it. "You have your phone?" he asked Rodney.

"Yeah."

"Take a picture of this," he said, pointing at the screen. Coleman opened the binder to a picture of the frail man. "And this."

"Okay," Rodney said, removing his phone. "But what this hafta do with what happened to yo—"

"It may show—um—what's the word? Negligence."

"I think it's cool," Rodney said, snapping a picture of the computer screen.

"Yeah, but look here," Coleman said, pointing at the binder.

Rodney craned toward the binder and squinted. He looked at the screen and squinted again. "Is that the same man?"

Coleman nodded with a crooked smile.

"Never mind. Not cool."

Rodney took a picture of the image in the binder.

"And here too," Coleman said, turning to the first page in the binder.

"CSHP1M3T," Rodney said as he snapped the picture. "Anything else?"

Coleman shook his head. "Not in here."

As he uttered those words, humming flowed from outside of the room. Footsteps accompanied the humming along the wall and toward the door. Coleman squatted behind the workbench with his crowbar clenched. Rodney ducked in a corner. Near the door, the footsteps and humming stopped simultaneously. Coleman and Rodney looked at each other. After a moment, the hums and walking continued away from the door and back along the wall.

"I think we should get outta here," Rodney said, standing.

Coleman stood and walked to Rodney. "Yeah, I think you should," he said on his way toward the door. He peeked out. There was no one in sight.

"What about you?"

"I'm not leaving until I find what I came for."

"But we don't even know if it's here."

"When I'm done checking this entire place, then I'll know."

Rodney sighed. "Let's find it."

Coleman nodded, then nudged the door open. Rodney followed as Coleman skulked to a crate. Coleman peeped around the container and saw the guard walking toward a hall at the opposite end of the building. Ten yards diagonally across the floor was a fishbowl room with frosted windows.

"This way," Coleman told Rodney while crouch-walking toward the room's glass door.

Coleman tugged the door handle, but it didn't open. "Locked."

Rodney pointed at a panel next to the door. "May need a card or electronic key or sumpin'."

Coleman looked at Rodney before turning his attention back to the door and patting the crowbar against his palm.

"Nah," Rodney said. "I know whatcha thinking. We can't break the door. It's glass. The guards'a be on us."

Coleman looked toward the hall where the guard disappeared. He glanced at the glass door, then pivoted and walked toward the hall.

"Where ya goin?" Rodney asked.

"To get a key."

Rodney shrugged, then shook his head and sighed.

Coleman hurried to the hallway entrance. Once there, he put his back against the corner and peeked into the hall. There were three doors. One on either side of the hall, and one at the end. But no sign of the guard.

Coleman winced. "Where'd he go?" he muttered as he stepped into the hall.

Before Coleman could take a second step, a toilet flush flowed from the door to his right. He quickly slipped back behind the wall. A few seconds later, the door opened and a loud yawn followed. Coleman peeked into the hall and saw the guard stretching his arms in the air and walking toward the opposite end of the hall. With his sights narrowed on the guard and his crowbar clutched, Coleman snuck behind the man. The guard pivoted and reached for his gun. But it was too late. Before the man could touch his gun, Coleman struck his hand with the crowbar. The guard hollered and clawed at Coleman with his other hand. Coleman parried his hand with the crowbar, then grasped the back of the guard's head and rammed the man's face into the wall. The man slumped to the floor unconscious. Coleman kneeled, searched him, and found a key fob clipped to his belt.

"You get a key?" Rodney asked as Coleman approached.

Coleman raised the fob at eye level. "Yep."

"Where'd you find it?"

"From the guard."

"Wait—you didn't?"

"Don't worry 'bout it. He's fine," Coleman said, waving the fob across the door's panel.

The door buzzed, and Coleman pulled it open. Inside, a rectangular workbench sat centered in the room. Behind the bench, on the back wall, was a metal shelf with small glass enclosures. Coleman quickly dodged around the workbench to the shelves.

"Whoa," Rodney said, as he gently closed the door behind himself and waited for it to auto lock. "That shelf has a lot of compartments."

Coleman placed the crowbar on top of the workbench. "No kiddin'. Help me look," he said, sliding a compartment's glass door up.

"Yeah—yeah," Rodney said, hustling to the opposite end of the shelf.

Inside, Coleman found a rack of six plastic test tubes with chemicals of varying colors in each. He grunted, then checked the compartment below it.

"What am I looking for?" Rodney asked.

"That poison being peddled as medicine."

"I know, but what it look like?"

"They're circle pills with CS406 on them," Coleman said while ransacking another compartment.

"Hey. Think I got it."

Coleman looked at Rodney, watching as his friend gazed at a pill bottle in his hand.

"You sure?" Coleman asked before snatching the bottle from Rodney.

Rodney shrugged. "You said CS406, right?"

Coleman didn't answer. He just inspected the pills inside the bottle and nodded. "Yeah. This is it. Where you find it?"

Rodney pointed to a compartment. "Here."

Coleman's eyes followed his friend's finger. "Anything else in there?" he asked, sliding the compartment's glass door open and finding a folded sheet of paper inside before Rodney could answer.

"What is it?" Rodney asked.

Coleman shook his head. "I don't know."

He opened the paper. CS406 sat boldly at the top of the page. Below was a circle graph, a bar graph, and numbers. Near the bottom, under the title RESULTS, was a phrase that gave Coleman both a feeling of relief and anger. *Confidence rate below 60%.*

"Look at this," he said to Rodney, flapping the sheet in the air between them. "They knew this crap wasn't close to a hundred percent, and they sold it anyway."

Rodney grabbed the paper and scanned it. Coleman put a hand over his own mouth and looked at the ground.

Rodney sighed. "Bro. I'm not a lawyer or anything, but I don't know if this is enough for a retrial or whatever."

Coleman looked at him.

"I mean, let's keep it and see what Tiffany says. But don't wanna get my hopes up, is all." Rodney placed the paper inside his pocket.

Coleman searched around the shelf. "There has to be more."

"We should get outta here."

At the bottom of the shelf, there was a larger compartment with a metal padlock door.

"There," Coleman said, pointing at the compartment.

He brushed past Rodney and snatched the crowbar from the workbench.

"I don't think that's a good idea. The guard—"

Coleman turned to Rodney on his way back to the shelf. "Look, if you wanna go, go. I'm not done yet, so watch out."

Rodney walked to the other side of the workbench while Coleman jammed his crowbar between the padlock's loop and pried at it until the lock snapped.

Coleman kneeled and opened the door. "Argh. Just more tubes of liquid," he said before standing and walking toward a desk near the back of the room. He searched through the stacks of paper on the desk but found nothing of significance to him.

"Yo, Tripp."

Coleman turned and saw Rodney kneeling at the shelf. He removed a slim, metallic container from the compartment and placed it on the workbench.

Coleman walked to his friend. "What is it?" he asked, laying his crowbar next to the container.

Rodney shrugged. "Not sure."

He reached to the container's side and unlatched it. Inside was a glass cylinder tube with a clear, reddish-brown fluid inside.

Coleman shook his head. "More of that liquid junk," he said, turning to the shelf and surveying the compartments.

"Hold up. This that metal-man juice."

"What?"

"That stuff they gave the man in the commercial to grow metal body parts. See." Rodney extended the tube to Coleman.

Coleman grabbed the tube and examined it. "This stuff can really do that?"

Footsteps rapidly approached the door. The door swung open, and a guard entered with his gun trained on Coleman and Rodney. Coleman reached for his crowbar, but before he could grab it, the guard fired a round. Rodney ducked. The bullet whizzed past, barely missing Coleman's shoulder before striking the back wall. Coleman stumbled and crashed to the floor.

"Don't move!" the guard demanded.

Coleman looked to his right and saw Rodney kneeled with his arms raised. As Coleman nudged himself from the floor, he felt a pain in his palm. The glass tube had broken and cut his hand. Coleman brushed and picked the glass from his palm. He grunted as the liquid from the broken tube trickled over his cuts and burned.

"Hands in the air!" the guard shouted.

Coleman felt a sharp pinch in his chest. He rubbed his hand across his chest and felt a piece of glass shard. He pulled it out and allowed it to fall to the floor. Some of the liquid from his hand dripped into the wound. Coleman winced at the sting.

"I said hands up!"

"Give em a sec. He's tryin'," Rodney said.

"Quiet," the guard barked as he circled the workbench, then stood seven feet away from Coleman and Rodney with his gun still trained on them.

Coleman pushed himself off the floor, and as he sat on his

heels, a pain ripped across his chest. Smoke rose from the lacerations on his chest and hand. Coleman hugged his upper body and fell to the floor again.

"Tripp," Rodney hollered, while dropping his arms and arching toward his friend.

"Stay back," the guard told him.

Rodney stopped and raised his hands. "He needs help!"

"Wh—what's happening to him?" the guard said.

"You need to call for help!"

Coleman's silver chain necklace softened around his neck. He touched it and found a metallic liquid on his finger. The necklace melted and oozed into the cut on his chest. It was as if the wound was sucking it in.

"I have a situation in Lab C," the guard said into his two-way radio. "Get in here now!"

Coleman lay on the floor, squirming and hollering in pain.

"Do something!" Rodney said to the guard.

"Quiet," the guard said.

A hard lump grew in Coleman's chest. Then another. Followed by another, and yet another. Coleman felt the lumps connecting as they crawled throughout his body. An agonizing pain overcame him. As Rodney and the guard argued, Coleman saw their lips moving but couldn't hear them. He briefly lost consciousness, but when he came to, he heard Rodney and the guard shouting.

Coleman jolted his head as the guard stepped around him towards Rodney. The man kept his gun on Rodney while lifting the stocky fellow to his feet and planting his face into the shelving.

"Hey, man," Rodney protested. "All you had to do was ask."

"Shut up," the guard said, patting Rodney down.

Rodney nodded to Coleman, who was still on the floor. "What about my homeboy?"

"Rod," Coleman struggled to say.

"You need to get him some help."

The guard shoved Rodney into the shelving. "I said shut up."

Coleman's eyes widened, and he clenched his fist. Immediately, a silver streak whacked the guard and sent him soaring toward the front door. A crashing sound followed by shattered glass hitting the floor echoed throughout the room. Coleman heaved himself from the floor and looked at Rodney.

Rodney stared back with his mouth agape. "Bro. Wh—what was that?" he finally asked.

"Huh? What are you talking about?" Coleman said, crawling to his knees.

He tried to stand but stumbled. Rodney caught him and helped him to his feet. Through a tear in Coleman's hoodie, Rodney saw chain links wrapped around his friend's upper body. They were the same design as the silver chain Coleman had.

Rodney pointed at the hoodie. "Your... you..."

Coleman looked at the hole in his hoodie. "Man, don't worry about that. I have a ton of these things," he said before breathing in, then slowly exhaling.

Rodney noticed the chain links absorb behind his friend's skin. He joggled his head and rubbed his eyes. "You know what? Let's get you outta here and to a hospital," he said.

Coleman shook his head. "No hospital. Let's just leave."

"Okay. Can you walk?"

"Yeah, I'm good."

They circled the workbench and moved toward the remnants of the door.

"What happened?" Coleman asked, glass crackling beneath his feet as he stepped through the hole where the door used to be.

Rodney shook his head. "Not exactly sure."

They stepped over the guard on the floor and hurried

across the warehouse toward the steel double door. When they were halfway there, the door opened, and a second guard entered. The man quickly removed his gun and pointed it at them.

Rodney ducked and raised his arms, but Coleman stood and glared at the guard. He felt anger mixed with a little fear. Coleman gritted his teeth, and as he did, chains wrapped around his head like cloth around a mummy.

The guard flinched at the sight and set his aim dead on Coleman. As Coleman lifted an arm to protect himself, a chain whipped from his forearm and spiraled into a circular shield. Four loud booms filled the air as bullets struck the shield before clanging to the floor. Coleman glanced at Rodney, who stared back with his mouth open. The shield unraveled, and the chain retracted back into Coleman's forearm as he lowered his arm.

"What—what the?" the guard said, the gun tottering in his shaky hands.

Coleman extended his palm toward the man, and a chain snapped from his hand. The guard dropped his gun and dove out of the chain's trajectory. The chain lashed past him and knocked over a barrel. Liquid leaked from the drum, and as the chain retracted, it sparked against the metal container.

CHAPTER SIX

BUSH HAD HIS fork in a slice of chocolate cake when he heard the explosion. The restaurant shook. Lisa, sitting across the table, looked at him with the white of her eyes exposed.

"What was that?" she asked, turning toward the restaurant's entrance.

Many other restaurant patrons gasped and yelped. The servers and staff dispersed throughout the floor to calm them.

"I'm sure it's nothing to worry about," Bush told Lisa, not believing it himself.

She looked at him with squinted eyes that seemed to ask, *are you serious?*

A waiter approached their table. "Sir, ma'am," he said. "Wanted to check and make sure you're okay."

Lisa nodded. "We are. Do you know what happened?"

"Not yet, but as soon as we find out, we'll let you know."

Lisa's phone rang. She looked at the screen, then at Bush. "I have to take this," she said to him before standing from the table.

Bush stood with her. "Okay, I'm gonna run to the restroom," he said.

Lisa walked toward the restaurant's bar, and Bush headed

toward the bathroom. He glanced in her direction to make sure she wasn't looking, then detoured through the kitchen, out the back door, and into a dark alley.

Bush clicked on his bracelet dials. "You guys heard that?" he asked.

Baadaye's voice entered his head. "Are you kiddin' me? The whole city heard it."

"We should investigate," Zamani said.

"Yep," Bush said, stepping back near a corner. "Let's do it."

The bracelets glowed, and Bush transformed into Zambaa before shooting into the star-glinted sky. Once he cleared the buildings, he saw smoke rising from near the warehouse yard just west of the city.

"That must be our place," Zamani commented.

"What gave it away? The cloud of smoke?" Baadaye said.

"Okay, let's make this quick, guys," Bush said. "I wanna get back to Lisa."

"Oh, boy."

Bush zoomed across the sky. Twenty seconds later, he arrived at the warehouse yard. It didn't take him long to find the smoking building.

"Half the wall is missing," Baadaye commented as Bush hovered above the structure.

"And there's still a fire," Bush said.

He dove toward the building and through the smoking hole before landing on a floor with crates and bins scattered around it. Bush quickly identified the spots where the fire spread and aimed his palms at the areas. Golden energy bubbles discharged from the gauntlets and smothered the flames. After a few seconds, the flames dissipated. Through the smoke, Bush saw someone sprawled on the floor. He zipped to the person and discovered a man dressed in a uniform covered with broken glass.

"He must be the guard," Bush said while kneeling next to the man. "Sir. Sir, are you okay?"

The man mumbled something and attempted to lift his head from the floor.

"No, no, no. Stay put until the medics arrive."

A rattling noise struck Bush's ear. He looked over his shoulder and stood. Squinting across the room, he saw the figure of another person lying on the floor.

"I'll be right back," Bush told the guard, before brushing his cloak to the side and floating toward the other individual.

Bush kneeled beside the short, stocky man. When he reached to check for a pulse, rattling and clanging flowed from behind him.

"Get away from him," a deep voice asserted.

Before Bush could fully stand and turn, a sturdy but flexible object struck his side and sent him crashing into a wooden crate. As Bush brushed the debris away and staggered to his feet, he heard more rattling.

"What was that?" Baadaye asked.

"I don't know," Bush said, jolting his head.

"Someone else is here, and they're strong," Zamani said.

Bush peered through the haze and saw a large, dark figure squatting near the short man on the floor.

"Hey," Bush shouted. "Whatta ya think you're doing?"

Bush took two steps in their direction. On his third step, the man-shaped contour stood and turned toward him.

"I said stay away," the figure growled in a demanding, eerie tone.

"I can't do that."

Before Bush could take his fifth step, a loud clangor slashed toward him, and a chain wrapped around his upper body.

Bush's eyes and mouth opened, and he gasped as the chain slammed him into a wall, then yanked him into the air and hammered him toward the floor. As Bush plummeted toward the concrete, he flicked his wrist at the dark figure and a ray of energy shot from his palm. The silhouette side-stepped the blast, and as he did, the chains around Bush loosened. Bush dropped to the floor, then quickly sprang to his feet and soared toward the figure. Halfway there, he felt a smack to his left side, followed by the sound of rattling chains. Bush crashed into a pile of bins, but immediately jumped to his feet and darted in the direction he had last seen the figure.

"Where'd he go?" Bush asked, standing where the mysterious man's silhouette once stood.

Thumping and chinking flowed from above. When Bush looked up, he saw the figure swinging through a hole in the roof.

"He's getting away," Baadaye said.

As Bush bent his knees to pursue, the stocky man on the floor groaned.

"He needs medical attention," Zamani said.

Bush looked at the man on the pavement next to him, then scanned the area. "Yeah. Let's get the injured outta here."

Five minutes later, Bush stood on the roof of a nearby warehouse watching as the police and ambulance surrounded the area. He had placed the short man and the guards outside on the ground in an area with plenty of light.

"We hafta find that guy," Baadaye said as the medics checked the men lying on the ground. "Before someone else gets hurt."

Bush nodded. "The only thing is, I didn't get a good look at him."

"He appeared to be a human with augmented abilities," Zamani said.

"He's definitely strong."

"Yeah, he did kick your butt," Baadaye said.

"Shut up. If you had a butt, he would have kicked yours too."

"If you plan on pursuing our unknown assailant tonight, perhaps you should inform your date," Zamani suggested.

"Oh, Lisa!" Bush said before launching into the sky.

It took him thirty seconds to make it to the restaurant and transform back into Calvin. Once inside, Bush walked to his table and found it empty. He looked around the room for Lisa, but there was no sign of her. On his way to the front entrance, he bumped into their waiter.

"My date," Bush said. "Have you seen her?"

"Oh, the young lady. I believe she left, sir."

"Great."

"Sorry."

Bush shook his head. "Not your fault. Can I get the check, please?"

"No need. She's already taken care of it."

Bush cocked his head to the side and lifted his arms before letting them drop to his outer thighs. "Okay, thank you. I guess," he said while removing his cellphone and exiting the restaurant. He saw he had some missed calls from Lisa and dialed her number. The phone rang four times before she answered.

"Where are you?" she asked.

"I was calling to ask you the same."

"You're the one who disappeared, dude."

Bush said nothing.

"I was worried about you, so I left looking for you."

"Well, I'm back at the restaurant. You're coming back?"

The line went silent for a beat.

"You know what? I think I'm just gonna head home."

"Hey Lisa. I'm sorry. Let's reschedule soon. The night was going well until—"

"Maybe. Just give me some time to think about it."

Bush sighed. "Okay, well, at least let me pay you back for dinner."

"No. It was my idea to have dinner, so don't worry about it. Talk to you later, Calvin."

"Yeah, later."

The call ended.

"She'll come around, Calvin," Zamani said.

"I'm not so sure," Bush said.

"Yeah, this isn't the first time you've flaked on her," Baadaye said.

"Not like I did it on purpose."

"I know. Just saying."

"Well, you're saying too much right now."

Bush clicked the dials on his beaded bracelet to off. Removing his phone, he poked at the screen, then held it to his ear.

"What's going on, bud?" Norman asked.

"Whatchu doing tonight?"

"You know me. Just hanging out with a few friends."

Bush did know Norm. And most of Norm's 'friends', he was pretty sure, were girls, which made Norm qualified in some areas but unqualified in others to give Bush advice on women.

"Where are you? I wanna hang."

"What! Lisa's letting you out?" Norman said.

"She doesn't let me do anything."

"Yeah, sure."

"You gonna tell me where you're at or not?"

Norman chuckled. "Of course, bud. Star Lounge."

CHAPTER SEVEN

THE STAR LOUNGE was a restaurant and game room situated downtown. It was a very popular evening spot for young professionals that under normal circumstances would have a line out of the building. Bush took a cab, and when he arrived, there was hardly anyone in line. It took him less than three minutes from the time he exited the taxi until he entered the establishment and found Norman sitting at a circular booth with a group. All women, except for one other guy. Bush recognized most of them as they worked in the same building.

"There he is," Norman said as Bush approached.

Bush fist bumped with Norman before turning to the rest of the group. "What's up, guys?"

Everyone from the group greeted him with a hello, a wave, a smile, or a combination of each.

"Hey, grab a seat," Norman said with a grin on his face. "I'll order you something to eat."

"Nah, I already ate. You think we can talk for a minute?"

Norman's smile flattened, and his eyebrows furrowed. "Sure thing. Give me a sec."

"Yep. Take your time. I'll be over here," Bush said, pointing at a small table to his left.

Norman nodded before turning to the group. Bush walked to the table and sat. A moment later, a waitress approached.

"Can I get you anything?" she asked.

Bush shrugged. "I ate earlier, so maybe just water."

The young lady cocked her head and smiled. "You sure? We have some of the best desserts."

"Chocolate cake?"

"Oh yeah. It's my favorite."

"Alright. I'll have water and a slice of your favorite chocolate cake."

"I'll get that in," the waitress said before glancing Bush over, then walking away.

Bush sat quietly, drumming his fingers on the table when Norman sat across from him.

"So, what's going on, bud?"

Bush looked at the floor. "I may regret this," he said, shaking his head.

"Huh? Regret what?"

"I think Lisa could be losing interest in me."

Norman winced. "What makes you think that?"

"Well, a lot of our dates have been cancelled or rescheduled."

"Uh-huh," Norman interjected while nodding.

"And what does 'uh-huh' mean?"

Norman shrugged. "You have been kinda flaky lately, bud."

Bush sighed. "Yeah, maybe you're right."

"But I see the way she looks at you—the way you look at each other. Trust me, she's not losing interest. But she may think you are."

Bush shook his head and looked away, giving consideration to what Norman just said. He thought about how his double life could send Lisa mixed messages. But he couldn't stop being Zambaa or tell her. Or could he? *No, it's way too dangerous,* Bush thought before looking at Norman.

"I can't believe I'm asking, but what's a good way to let her know I'm interested?" Bush asked.

Norman shrugged. "You know women like Lisa enjoy gifts, flowers, picnics in the park, and all that stuff."

"You don't sound too sure."

"Well, Lisa's different from the girls I date."

Bush chuckled. "Yeah, that's a good point."

"But I do know something all women want."

"Yeah, what's that?"

"To know they have your undivided attention."

Bush nodded.

"Here you go," the waitress said, while placing a glass of water and a plate with a slice of chocolate cake on the table. "A water and my favorite cake."

"Thank you," Bush said.

The waitress stared at him for a moment then smiled. Bush returned the smile.

"Let me know if I can get anything else for you," she said before walking away.

"What's up with that?" Norman asked.

"Oh, I had dinner earlier but didn't get a chance to finish dessert."

"No, no. I mean the look the waitress gave you."

"Don't start, Norm."

Norman hunched his shoulders. "I'm just sayin'," he said before laughing.

Bush unwrapped a fork from a napkin on the table and cut into his cake. As he chewed the soft, buttery, silky treat, Norman waved to someone walking past.

"Hey, Michelle," Norman called.

A woman wearing a black midi dress and dirty blonde hair in a teased ponytail approached the table. Following behind her was a woman in a skirt and blazer. She had short, natural curly hair and almond skin.

"What's up, Norman?" the woman in the midi dress asked.

"You're leaving already?" Norman asked.

"Yeah," she said, pointing her thumb over her shoulder at the woman with the curly hair behind her. "Catching a ride with my friend. She works close to where I live."

"Michelle," the woman in the skirt suit said. "If you need to stay, you can. Imma get out of here."

Norman peeked around Michelle. "And who are you, beautiful?" he asked the woman with the curly hair.

She scoffed, then contorted her lips before saying, "Tiffany."

"Hi, Tiffany. I'm Norman, and this is my friend, Calvin. Calvin, meet Michelle and Tiffany."

Bush swallowed the cake in his mouth and nodded at the two women. "Hello ladies," he said.

They both acknowledged him with a smile and a hello.

"Your friend's cute," Michelle told Norman.

"Hear that, Calvin?" Norman said. "Michelle thinks you're cute."

Bush half grinned but said nothing.

"Michelle, I hafta go, girl," Tiffany said.

"Oh, yeah, okay, okay," Michelle said to her before turning to Norman. "We have to get outta here."

Norman shrugged. "Why the big hurry?"

"Tiff has work to do—you know, since she's a lawyer and all."

Tiffany cocked her head and stared at Michelle.

Norman winced. "Work? Now?"

"Something dealing with that explosion earlier, right Tiff?"

Bush glanced at Tiffany.

"Yeah," Tiffany said while pointing her thumb toward the entrance.

"And like I said, we're catching a ride together. Nice meeting you, Calvin," Michelle said.

"Good meeting you both," Tiffany immediately followed up as the women turned away.

Bush threw a hand in the air. "Same here."

"Hate to see you ladies leave," Norman said.

"Bye, Norman," Michelle yelled back in a playful tone.

"Whatta shame," Norman said. "Working on a Friday night. Happy I'm not a lawyer."

Bush shrugged, then took a sip of water.

"You're done?" Norman asked. "There's some more people I'd like you to meet."

"Girls?"

Norman didn't speak, but the smile on his face answered Bush's question.

"Nah," Bush said. "I'm gonna get outta here."

"What? You too?"

Bush stood. "Yep," he said, placing some money on the table.

Norman sighed. "Alright, bud," he said, standing.

The two fist bumped.

"I'll catch ya later," Bush said before leaving his friend, threading around a table then a crowd on his way to the entrance.

Outside, Bush immediately spotted Tiffany at the curb, ducking into the back seat of a car after Michelle. Bush turned his bracelet dials on.

"You guys with me?" Bush murmured.

"Of course," Zamani's voice said in his head.

"Oh, now you want to talk to us?" Baadaye said.

"Baadaye, chill," Bush said. "We have a situation."

"Is this about Lisa? Like your womanizing friend said, let her know she has your attention."

"I believe he's referring to the young lawyer lady,"

Zamani said. "Her work is connected to the incident earlier this evening."

"Thank you, Zamani," Bush said. "Good to know someone was paying attention."

"Yeah, yeah," Baadaye said. "What's the plan?"

The ladies' car slowly veered into traffic.

"We're going to follow them," Bush said, hiking along the sidewalk to the west end of the building.

He darted down a side street before dodging around a delivery truck and into a dark corner. A few moments later, Bush floated in the sky as Zambaa. He quickly spotted the car flowing with traffic and pursued at an inconspicuous distance from the sky. After twelve minutes of coasting, stopping at lights, and turning, the car parked near a curb in front of a ten-story apartment building. Bush perched on the building's top ledge and watched as Michelle exited the car. She waved to the vehicle, then walked toward the building. When she made it inside, the car eased back into traffic.

Bush followed the vehicle for another half mile before the car slowed and parked at another building, a twenty-story office building with two pairs of double-glass doors at the entrance. Bush landed on a rooftop across the street. A moment later, Tiffany stood from the car and walked to the building's entrance. She removed something from her pocket and waved it across a small panel next to the door. She entered, and the door hung open. Bush made sure no one was around, then quickly swooped down to the side of the building and transformed into Calvin before darting to the door and catching it before it closed. He entered a large, empty lobby. To his left, a sitting area led into a hall. His right, a cafe restaurant. In front of him, an unoccupied security desk and Tiffany's back as she walked toward the elevators. Bush hurried to his left and took cover behind a wall. He looked up and noticed a camera.

"Oh, the cameras," he said.

"Already taken care of," Zamani said.

"You're covered," Baadaye said in sync.

Bush sighed. For a moment he forgot the gauntlets, even in bracelet form, released an aura of energy around him when he was on stealth missions or transforming between Calvin and Zambaa. That energy caused nearby cameras and video recorders to show blurry images or static.

"Thanks," Bush said, peeking around the corner.

Tiffany pressed the elevator panel, then stood back. She looked in Bush's direction, but he quickly ducked back behind the wall. The elevator dinged, then opened. Bush peeked and saw the elevator door closing. He hurried to the elevators and arrived just in time to hear the car thump and hum into motion. Tracking the glowing numbers on the elevator's panel, Bush noticed number sixteen was the last to illuminate. He pressed the up arrow and waited. A door closing from the hall flowed through the area. Footsteps approached the lobby, but Bush didn't see anyone. A moment later, a security guard emerged from the hall. The elevator door behind Bush dinged and opened. Bush immediately entered and pressed the button for the sixteenth floor.

"That was close," Baadaye commented.

"Yeah, it was," Bush said.

The elevator went to the sixteenth floor without stopping. Bush exited and entered a dim hallway. The sound of heels clicking flowed from his left. He crept in that direction and made another left at the corner. Tiffany entered a door at the end of the hall. In a crouch, Bush hurried toward the door, hoping to catch it before it closed.

"I'm not gonna make it," he grumbled.

"Gotcha," Baadaye said as a faint stream of golden light discharged from his bracelet and illuminated the door.

The door remained open for two extra seconds, giving Bush enough time to reach it.

"Thanks," he said, stepping into a receptionist area.

Directly in front of Bush sat a receptionist desk with a large plaque above it. "Keller and Raven," Bush said aloud.

A thump came from the right and Bush crouched-walked in that direction. It led him into a hall with offices on either side. The hall quickly flowed into a floor with empty cubicles. Bush followed the clatter to a corner office. He peeked inside and saw Tiffany's back as she rummaged through a filing cabinet. A vibration ranged from her desk. Bush tracked the noise to a glowing cell phone. As Tiffany turned toward the phone, Bush ducked back into the hall and pressed his back against the wall.

"Hi," Tiffany said into the phone. "Yeah, yeah, I know. Had to come to the office and get the file on Sharpe, but I'll meet you there shortly. Right. I heard Rodney Garrison was at the facility during the explosion. Yeah, from what I'm told, he's now at The Hart Medical Center in police custody. Uh-huh. Tripp Coleman. He may have been, I'm not sure—look, I'm getting the file now, I'll be on my way. Yep, yep, okay, see you soon."

A moment later, the filing cabinet closed, and Tiffany's heels clicked toward the door. With his back against the wall, Bush shuffled to an empty office on his right and hid behind the desk inside. He watched as Tiffany walked past, exhaling as she did. Bush waited until he no longer heard her footsteps before leaving the office and walking to the receptionist's area. He exited the door and took the hallway toward the elevator. When he reached the end of the hall, he heard the elevator door thump closed. He glanced around the corner to make sure it was clear before walking past the elevators to the stairwell and taking it to the roof.

"Are you planning on paying this Rodney Garrison a visit tonight?" Zamani asked when they arrived on the rooftop.

Bush shook his head. "Not tonight," he said as he slowly morphed into Zambaa. "He's probably still recovering, and

I'm sure the cops have lots of questions for him. It'd be difficult for me to get any information from him now."

"Can't wait too long," Baadaye said. "There's a buff dude out there somewhere."

"An augmented human," Zamani said.

"Yeah whateva."

Bush nodded. "I'll go in the morning," he said before jetting into the star dotted sky.

CHAPTER EIGHT

THE NEXT MORNING, Tripp Coleman opened his eyes and found himself sprawled on a floor. Food wrappers, clothing, and dust bunnies lay with him. As Coleman pushed himself to his knees, the old wooden floor creaked. He cracked his neck and stretched his arms before dragging himself to a nearby sofa and sitting. Resting his face in his palms, Coleman moaned at the throbbing inside of his head.

"Hold on," he said, standing from the sofa and inspecting his hands.

His hands looked normal, with all five fingers intact. He hurried to the bathroom and studied his reflection in the mirror. His face looked normal. The bump on his forehead and the black eye he received from the police were gone.

"It was a dream?" he questioned on his way back into the living area. Coleman examined the tears in his hoodie and jeans. "Was it?"

His stomach growled, and he rushed to the kitchen with an overwhelming desire for food. Grabbing a bundle of three spotted bananas, he quickly unpeeled each and scarfed them down in less than a minute. He then raided the cabinets until he found a box of cereal. Upending the box, he caught as many of the small circles in his mouth as he could, allowing the others to fall on the countertop and floor. Once the box was empty, Coleman crunched across the cereal on the floor, opened the refrigerator, and removed a bowl with leftover rice he had from take out. He cuffed his hand and shoveled the rice into his mouth. After the second load, the craving stopped.

Coleman closed the refrigerator door and placed the bowl on the countertop. "What was that?" he asked himself on his way into the living room.

He plopped on the sofa and rested his forehead in his palms. His palms moved down his face, and he wiped his eyes with his fingers. Glancing at a shelf next to the sofa, a framed picture caught his eye. Coleman stood and walked to the shelf before grabbing the picture. The image contained a woman and a man standing with a little boy between them.

"Miss you two," he said, resting the picture back on the shelf and picking up another picture next to it.

In the photo, a gray-haired woman sat in a chair. A younger Coleman squatted next to the chair with an arm around her.

"Wish you were here," he said.

Coleman sat the picture back down and noticed a third photo of him and Rodney with boxing gloves on, goofing off in a gym.

"Rodney."

As Coleman uttered those words, a vibration came from the floor. He looked and saw his cell phone halfway under the sofa. Coleman grabbed the phone and pressed at the busted screen. He had multiple missed calls and text messages. The most recent text message said. *It's Tiffany. Where are you? You need to call me back now.* Just as he finished reading the text, tires screeching flowed from the front of the house. Coleman peeked through the front window and saw three police cars on the street. A group of officers exited the cars and entered the front yard with hands on their firearms. Coleman hurried to the opposite end of the house. Opening a slit in the window blinds next to the back door, he peeped through the window and saw two more officers approaching with their guns aimed at the house.

Three brisk knocks came from the front door, and Coleman stepped into the living area just in time to hear, "Tripp Coleman! It's the police. Open up!"

Coleman froze for a moment, weighing his options. None of which looked good. After a moment, he removed his torn shirt and hoodie, and grabbed a clean shirt from a laundry basket on the floor. While he shrugged into the fresh shirt, two more knocks banged at the door.

"Tripp Coleman!"

"Comin'!" Coleman yelled.

He took a deep breath before walking to the door and unlocking it. With the door ajar, Coleman peeked outside. An officer with dark hair stood in front of the door. A taller officer stood behind him to his right, a chubby officer to his left.

"How can I help you, officer?" Coleman asked.

"You can stand back and let us in."

"For what?"

The officer scoffed and shook his head. "Not that I hafta answer that, but there was a break-in last night."

Coleman shrugged.

"We suspect you might've been involved. Now, stand back from the door."

"Do you have a warrant?"

"We don't need a warrant out here," the chubby officer interjected.

"To come in here, you do."

"What was that?" the chubby officer said, stepping forward.

"Have a good day, officers," Coleman said while nudging the door forward to shut it.

The dark-haired officer placed his foot in front of the door and stopped it from closing, and the chubby officer shoved the door while the taller cop unholstered his pistol.

Coleman pushed against the door. "What'chall doing? You don't have a warrant."

"I said we don't need one in this neighborhood."

Coleman overpowered the officers, then immediately shut, and locked the door. He heard an officer yell something toward the back of the house. A second later, a loud thump came from the front door. A similar noise followed from the back, as the house's walls and floor vibrated and tremored. The front door flung open, and the three officers came in with their guns trained on Coleman. Shortly after, a crash came from the back of the house and two more policemen crowded into the living area.

The tall officer grabbed Coleman and forced his arms behind his back. The chubby officer hurried over and pushed Coleman to the floor.

Coleman fell to his belly. "You need a warrant. You can't do this!"

"Looks like we can," the chubby officer said.

"This is my grandmother's house!"

"I don't care!" the chubby officer asserted as his taller partner cuffed Coleman's hands.

Coleman felt heat rise from his stomach to his throat. Cold, metallic chains swathed his entire body like bandages. The handcuffs popped from his wrists and chains from his chest pushed him from the floor and onto his feet, knocking the chubby and tall officers to the floor. The two police officers who entered through the back stared at Coleman with wide eyes and gaped mouths. Coleman flung his hands at them, and two chains whipped from his arms, striking the two men and sending them crashing into the back wall.

A loud boom stuffed the room, and Coleman felt an object hit the metallic covering between his right temple and jaw. He turned to find the dark-haired officer gawking with his smoking gun aimed at the chain-shrouded man. Coleman pointed his hand at the policeman while slightly closing his fist. A chain lashed from his arm and wrapped around the officer's upper body. The chain heaved the man up into the ceiling, then dropped him to the floor as broken wood and debris fell on top of him. The tall officer crawled toward his gun. Coleman soccer kicked him through the front door and across the yard. Two more blasts echoed through the house, and Coleman felt two bullets ricochet off his back as he pivoted to the chubby officer, who stood staring with his mouth wide open.

Coleman raised his hand toward the man, then made a fist. A chain whipped around the officer's neck before lifting him from the floor. The policeman immediately dropped his pistol and clenched the chain around his neck.

"Wha—what are you?" he asked struggling to get the words out.

Coleman stepped close to the man, and as he did, the officer peed on himself.

"Pathetic," Coleman growled before directing the chain to smack the chubby man against the wall twice, then slinging him to the floor.

Coleman surveyed the carnage throughout the house. On the floor, in a now busted frame, he spotted the picture of him and the older lady. The chains covering Coleman disappeared into his skin as he kneeled and snatched the picture from the frame. Sirens wailed in the distance. Coleman stood and placed the photo in his pocket before removing his second torn shirt for the day. Stepping over one officer, he removed a hoodie from the laundry basket on his way to the back door. Once outside, he threw on the hoodie, zipped it up, and flipped the hood over his head.

Coleman walked four blocks to a bus stop. The inside of the bus was sparse, with only the driver and three other passengers sitting up front. Coleman walked to the back and removed his phone to call Tiffany.

"Where are you?" she asked when she answered the phone.

"The cops came to my house."

"No kiddin'."

"They knocked down the door without a warrant."

"Well, that's not legal, but you're wanted for questioning concerning that explosion last night."

Coleman said nothing.

"You have to turn yourself in."

"No, not yet."

"What do you…" Tiffany raised her voice but paused. Her heels clicking against the floor echoed through the phone, followed by a door opening, then shutting. "You gotta turn yourself in. Rodney's in the hospital under police custody."

"What? Is he okay? Where?"

"He's fine. Just banged up a bit. Hart Medical Center."

"He's okay? You sure?"

"Yes. I need you to go to the nearest police station. Let me know where."

Coleman shook his head at the phone. "Did you get the documents from Rodney?"

"What documents?"

"See if you can find his clothes—also copy the pictures from his phone."

"Wait. So, you were at that facility?"

"Sharpe is involved with some shady stuff."

"I know that, but there's a—"

"We have something I think you can use."

Tiffany sighed. "Alright, alright. I'll see if I can locate Rodney's things. But you need to turn yourself in. Call me to let me know where you're at before you do. Okay?"

"I will when it's time," Coleman said before ending the call.

He rode the bus to a subway station, then took the train to downtown. After a silent twenty-minute ride and a five-block hike, Coleman arrived at the Hart Medical Center. With his hood on, he entered through the automatic sliding doors and dodged a man and nurse on his way to the front desk. A petite lady stood behind the desk, staring into a binder. Coleman removed his hood as he approached.

"Excuse me," he said.

The lady looked at him. "Yes," she said, smiling.

"I'm here to see Rodney Garrison."

She nodded. "Alright." The lady clicked her mouse and tapped at her keyboard. "You said Rodney Gerald?"

"Garrison. Rodney Garrison."

"Ah, okay, I see him. Who did you say you are?"

"A friend and coworker."

"He's in room five thirty-two but not currently taking visitors."

"Any reason why?"

The lady shrugged. "Doctor's orders," she said.

"Really wanted to see him. He doesn't have a lot of family in the area."

"I see. Well, come back tomorrow or try calling his room later."

Coleman glanced toward the elevators and saw a guard scanning the lobby. He turned his attention back to the woman. "I'll do that," he said before pivoting away and walking toward the entrance. Instead of going to the doors, Coleman made a left and darted into a hall. He entered the door for the stairwell and took it to the fifth floor. Hospital staff and visitors paced about the area. A nurses' station sat at the center of the floor. Coleman spotted a guard at the station talking to a pretty nurse. Raising a hand to his forehead, Coleman covered his face and turned toward the wall on his right. Arrows on the wall indicated room five thirty-two was on the opposite end of the floor, past the guard.

Rubbing his forehead, Coleman walked by the guard and nurse, seemingly unnoticed. He continued into a hall and found room five thirty-two midway. The door was open, so Coleman peeked inside. He saw Rodney in the room alone. The stocky fellow lay in a hospital gown, handcuffed to the bed. He had a few cuts on his arms and some minor bruising on his face. As Coleman stepped toward the room's door, he felt a hand grab his bicep then pull him back toward the hall. He turned and saw Tiffany's curly hair as she guided him across the hallway and into a room with two empty beds.

"I thought I was clear when I said you should turn yourself in to the police," she said in a hushed tone. "Why are you here?" Tiffany winced as she stared at Coleman's face. "You heal fast."

The intercom buzzed and paged a doctor to the second floor.

"I came to check on my boy," Coleman said.

"Tripp, you're making this very difficult."

"I told you I'll turn myself in when it's time. Did you get Rodney's things?"

"Not yet. We spoke less than an hour ago."

Coleman shook his head. "You need to get them now."

"And you need to get out of here now. C'mon," Tiffany said, while pulling Coleman by the arm.

Coleman yanked his arm away. "Tiffany," he said as they stood in the hall. "Get them."

She looked into his eyes. "Tripp, what happened?" she asked, placing a hand on his shoulder.

He shook his head. "I can't go unless I have your word," he said.

"I—I promise," she said. "I'll go check now, but you should get outta here and go to the police. You saw what they did to you for standing in the wrong place at the wrong time. Imagine what they'll do now that you're wanted."

Coleman glanced at the floor and clenched his fist. "Yeah, I remember," he said, looking at Tiffany. "But they couldn't hurt me now if their lives depended on it."

Tiffany's eyebrows furrowed. She opened her mouth to say something, but before she could speak, footsteps, followed by a voice, came from up the hall.

"Excuse me," said a pale man wearing a suit and glasses. "Are you Ms. Stephens, the lawyer?"

Next to the man stood a bald, bulky guy who also wore a suit. Coleman squinted at the sight of the muscular man. He seemed familiar to him. Behind the men were two more men in tactical gear, both wearing pistols on their hips.

Tiffany paused, her eyes dancing as she studied the men. "Yes, that's me," she answered. "How can I help you?"

"I'm Agent Beckett with the FBI," the pale man said. "We were told the terrorist who attacked the research facility last night is on this floor. You're representing him?"

Tiffany winced. "I'm sorry," she said, shaking her head. "Who did you say you were with?"

"FBI; we're investigating the terrorist attack last night."

Coleman looked the muscular man up and down.

"I don't believe it was a terrorist attack," Tiffany told Beckett.

"What would you call it?" Beckett asked.

Tiffany shrugged. "I don't know. Could've been an accident. Does Sharpe keep flammable substances in his research facility?" she said, dragging out the words research facility.

Beckett chuckled.

"What room is the suspect in?" the bulky man asked.

Coleman studied the guy's face as he spoke.

Beckett pointed at Coleman. "And who's this?" he asked.

Tiffany lifted her chin and her eyes rolled up and to the left. "You're asking a lot of questions, but how do you know me, and not know the name of your so-called terrorist? Because if you knew his name, you wouldn't be asking for his room number. Can I see your badges?"

Coleman grimaced as he remembered where he saw the muscular man. "You work for Sharpe, don't you? I saw you at the hearing," Coleman said to the muscular guy.

Beckett and the bulky man glanced at one another.

"Tell us where he is," Beckett asserted.

Coleman stepped in front of Tiffany and nudged her behind himself.

"Bad idea," the bulky man said.

The guards behind Beckett and the muscular man aimed their pistols at Coleman. Tiffany screamed.

"You two are coming with us," Beckett said.

Coleman set his jaw and glared at the men.

CHAPTER NINE

GUNFIRE ROARED FROM the hospital as Bush stood across the street.

"Oh my," Zamani said.

"Looks like we've arrived just in time for the party," Baadaye commented.

Passersby near the hospital ducked, while individuals inside exited and hurried away from the building. Bush raced into the parking garage behind him, then into its stairwell. Once he was clear, he transformed into Zambaa and soared from the garage toward the hospital. Halfway there, a window on the fifth floor shattered and a hollering man in tactical gear plunged toward the ground. Bush swooped in and caught the man at the second-floor level.

"What's going on?" Bush asked as he settled the man on the ground.

The man ignored the question. He glanced up at the fifth floor, then whimpered and ran away.

"We gonna let him leave?" Baadaye asked.

"Yeah, I think we have bigger issues," Bush said before hovering toward the busted window.

He entered what appeared to be a break room. A refrigerator lay on the vinyl flooring, joined by flipped tables and chairs. The fire alarm blared, and people ran and screamed throughout the floor.

"Not good," Zamani commented.

More gunfire rang from outside the break room. Bush zipped through the opening where the door used to be and couldn't believe what he saw at the end of the hall. Another man dressed in tactical gear was halfway through the stairwell door, but a chain restrained his upper body. The chain connected to a man who had chains wrapped around his entire body. He slung his hand, and the man in the tactical gear crashed into the wall on the opposite side of the hallway. As the man in the tactical gear crawled to his feet, the chain-wrapped man towered over him with his hand raised. A chain whipped from the man's arm and Bush bolted toward him, catching the chain midair.

The chain-swathed man looked over his shoulder and growled. "The hero," he said.

"Who are you?" Bush asked.

The man in tactical gear staggered to his feet, opened the stairwell door, and hurried into the stairwell. A second chain whipped from the chain-man's arm and smacked Bush, sending the hero stumbling backward.

"They're getting away," the chain man said on his way to the stairwell door.

Bush darted behind the chain-slinging man and put him into a full nelson hold.

"Get off of me," said the chain-wrapped man while struggling, "They have her."

"Who?" Bush asked. "Calm down before someone gets hurt."

"The only person getting hurt is you. I said, let me go!"

The man headbutted Bush before wrapping a chain around the hero and throwing him up to the ceiling, then down to the floor.

"He's a lot stronger than I anticipated," Zamani commented.

"Yeah, but he's not stronger than us," Baadaye said. "Let's hit him with an energy blast, C.B."

Bush shook his head. "Don't wanna risk hurting bystanders," he said, crawling to one knee.

"Perhaps it'd be better if this fight was conducted outside," Zamani said.

"Perhaps," Bush said, watching as the chain-swaddled man opened the stairwell door.

Before he could walk through, Bush aimed his palm at the man, and three golden energy bands shot from the gauntlet. The first band wrapped around the man's shoulders, the second restrained his hands to his waist, and the third tethered his ankles together. The chain-wielding man fell to his side.

"See how you like being tied up," Baadaye said.

Bush pointed his hand at the chain man and a golden aura encircled the man as he squirmed on the floor. With the chain-wrapped man floating behind him, Bush quickly soared to the break room, and through the busted window he had used to enter the hospital. Bush jetted through the sky while the chain man struggled in the energy bubble behind him.

"Not good," Baadaye said as the chain-swaddled man broke the band around his shoulders. "He is pretty strong."

Bush looked back and saw the man tearing through the energy band around his waist.

"Careful," Zamani warned as Bush flew toward a skyscraper.

"Whoa!" Bush exclaimed, skirting by the building.

Bush felt a cold, hard object around his legs. When he looked back, he saw his legs chained together and the chain-swathed man flying toward him. Bush twisted to face the man. The two collided, then exchanged blows as they plunged toward Millennium Park. Bush hit the chain-wrapped man with an energy blast as they crashed into the pavement near the Cloud Gate Bean. Debris peppered the area, and a veil of dust formed. People screamed while running and clearing the area. Lying inside the cratered pavement, Bush moaned and jolted his head.

"Rough landing," Baadaye commented.

"Yeah, well, at least we're outta the hospital," Bush said.

"Stay vigilant," Zamani said as rattling chains echoed toward them.

The remaining debris and dust from crushed concrete cleared, and the chain-swaddled man stood in its place.

"Let's take him," Baadaye said.

"Easier said than done," Bush said. "This guy hits hard, and I have to be careful with my energy blast. There's still people around."

Sirens wailed in the distance.

"I think we may have a solution," Zamani said.

At that, the gauntlets glowed, and ridges formed around the fingers and knuckles.

"This should even the odds."

"Yeah, he'll definitely feel your punches now," Baadaye added.

Bush stood and examined the gauntlets. "You guys always have a trick up your sleeves—or cuffs rather," he said before setting his jaw on the chain man.

The man charged toward Bush with a punch. Bush ducked and delivered a hook to the man's midsection, then followed up with a cross to his jaw. As the chain-shrouded man stumbled backward, he flicked his wrist, and a chain snapped from his hand and wrapped around Bush's neck. The man wrenched the chain, and Bush dropped to one knee.

"Because of you they have her!" the chain-wrapped man said.

Bush tugged at the chain around his neck. "Have who?" he struggled to ask.

The man gripped the chain and positioned his body for another pull, but before he could, Bush grabbed the chain and yanked it. As the chain-wielding man staggered toward him, Bush stood and delivered a direct blow to the man's chest. The impact sent the chain-shrouded man soaring through the air, then tumbling across the pavement.

"Direct hit," Zamani said.

"That was nice, C.B.," Baadaye said.

"It's not over yet," Bush said.

Chains rattled as the chain-swathed man stood to his feet. "Boy, you asking for me to stomp my foot in yo behind," he said.

"Don't know who you are, but I don't wanna hurt you," Bush said.

The man smirked. "How?" he said, shrugging with his palms toward the sky. "I'm practically indestructible. And you can call me… Tripp Chain."

Bush shook his head.

"Haven't pushed myself to see what I'm really capable of," Tripp Chain continued. "Let's see." He placed his palms together, then cuffed his hands. Multiple chain links wound and clanked from his arms and formed a ball of chains.

Bush's eyes widened as the ball grew larger by the second. When the orb expanded to the size of the Atwood Sphere, the chain-wrapped man axed his hands and the large ball spiraled toward Bush.

"Incoming," Zamani warned.

Bush aimed his palms at the giant, metallic ball and golden energy beams discharged from his hands. The energy blast knocked the sphere back in Tripp Chain's direction. Chains whipped from his arms and chest and connected to the large metal orb. He caught the ball with the chains, but the impact sent his heels crushing through the pavement. He slid backward ten yards before stopping and dropping the sphere. The large ball smashed to the pavement, creating an enormous crater in the concrete beneath it.

"Yeah, he's strong," Baadaye commented.

"You think?" Bush said.

Tripp Chain glared at Bush, then dropped to one knee and panted.

Bush's eyebrows furrowed. "Huh. Maybe he's reached his limit."

A police squad car darted from the main road, then swerved onto the pavement. Two armed policemen exited the car and aimed their guns at the chain-swaddled man.

"Hands in the air," one officer commanded.

Tripp Chain stood and turned toward the officers with his hands raised.

"Now walk toward us, slowly," the officer continued.

"These guys can't be serious," Baadaye said.

"Perhaps he's overexerted and ready to turn himself in," Zamani followed up.

As the chain-wrapped man stepped toward the cop car, a chain snapped from his chest and struck one officer, knocking the policeman to the ground.

"Or maybe not," Bush said, soaring toward the chain-wielding man.

The other officer fired a round. The bullet ricocheted off Tripp Chain's shoulder. He pointed his hand at the officer, and a chain whipped from his fist, knocking the gun from the policeman's hands.

As Bush swooped in, Tripp Chain smacked him with a chain from his free hand. Bush crashed to the pavement but quickly sprang to his feet. When he did, he found Tripp Chain facing him.

"Help me," the officer cried out, suspended in the air with a chain wrapped around his upper body.

Tripp Chain grinned at Bush. "You're just a pet for the

cops and this bias system," he said. "So go fetch!" Tripp Chain coiled the chain, then flung the officer.

Bush's eyes widened and his mouth gaped as the policeman hollered and flopped from a hundred feet in the air. Swishing into the sky, Bush caught him. The officer continued to scream as they descended toward the ground.

"My, my. He's a lively one," Zamani said inside of Bush's head.

"Okay dude, you're saved," Baadaye said.

Bush set the officer on the pavement, then looked around for Tripp Chain. He was gone.

"Are you okay?" Bush asked the officer.

The man nodded. "Yeah, yeah, I think so," he said.

Bush walked to the other officer. The man sat on the ground, palming the side of his head.

"You okay?" Bush asked him.

The man slowly nodded, then gestured with a thumbs up.

"Okay. Try not to move too much until the paramedics come."

Bush walked to an empty area, then rocketed into the sky and toward the hospital. He entered through the same window he did originally. The inside was still hectic, but there was a noticeable orderly purpose compared to before. Bush passed through the break room and into the hall. A group of nurses and doctors stood talking. The stress was apparent on most of their faces. As Bush walked toward them, they all turned to him, many with their mouth gaped, others google-eyed, and some both.

"Rodney Garrison?" Bush asked.

Everyone in the group pointed down the hall. "Room— room five thirty-two," a nurse said.

"Thank you," Bush said before continuing up the hall.

He entered the room and found a short, stocky guy lying handcuffed to a bed.

"Rodney Garrison?" Bush asked as he entered.

Rodney squinted at Bush. "Wait, you, you, you're," he said, struggling to get it out.

"I know. Now, I need you to tell me everything."

For seven minutes, Rodney shared how he and Coleman snuck into Sharpe's research facility. He explained everything, including the explosion and where he lost consciousness.

"So, your friend, Tripp Coleman is this Tripp Chain?" Bush asked.

"Tripp Chain? Yeah, I mean, I guess," Rodney said.

"Whatta ya mean, you guess?"

"It's not Tripp's fault. He needs help."

"That's an understatement," Baadaye grumbled inside Bush's head.

"Maybe not completely his fault, but you guys did break and enter. I'm still unclear why," Bush told Rodney.

Rodney scoffed, then shook his head. "Sharpe's a crook, aight."

"Why were you guys looking for those pills? The CC—whatever?"

"The CS406."

"Yeah."

"Look, Tripp doesn't like me telling people about this—"

"We're past that. Innocent people could get hurt."

"Man, don'tcha think I know that?" Rodney said before sighing, then looking at the bed's footboard. "When Tripp was a teenager," he continued, slowly lifting his head and looking at Bush. "Both his parents were killed in a robbery, so he went to live with his grandma. She raised him and kept him outta trouble for the most part." Rodney paused, then smiled. "We used to go to the gym and box. Kept us off the streets, you know." His smile angled downward. "But during our senior year in high school, Tripp's grandma got sick, and they needed money. So, Tripp went to the streets and did what he had to." Rodney looked at Bush. "You know what I mean. You seem like an around the way brotha. Or are you from a different planet that has black people? Are you from a different planet? Cause I was reading a book that said black people could—"

Bush patted the air between him and Rodney. "Calm down. I know what you mean. Go on."

Rodney shrugged. "Anyway. Tripp was able to get his grandma the medicine and treatment she needed. She started getting better, but street life caught up with Tripp, and he got arrested." Rodney paused and shook his head. "Don't understand how the cops arrested him but couldn't catch the people that robbed and killed his parents. It's a shame. Anyhow, without Tripp working the streets, his grandma couldn't afford the good medicine, so she went with the cheaper generic stuff."

"CS406?"

"Yep. Sharpe's company had cheap medicine for her condition. It was what she could afford at the time, but she got more sick. That medicine wasn't even fully ready."

"How you know that?"

"We found results at the research facility."

"Really?"

"Yeah. We found some pictures of that chemical that got on Tripp too."

"Did you keep them?"

Rodney stared at Bush but said nothing.

"I need to know, so I can help your friend and put Sharpe on blast before someone else gets hurt."

Rodney continued to stare at the hero. After a moment, the stocky man exhaled, then reached for the nightstand drawer next to his bed. The cuffs around his other wrist clanked.

"Ouch," Rodney growled.

"Wait," Bush said. "Where's it at? I'll get it."

"Top drawer. Under my clothes, there's a cellphone and sheet of paper."

Bush aimed his palm at the nightstand, then rotated his hand as if he was turning a doorknob. The nightstand drawer slid open, and Rodney's clothes creased forward. Glowing with a golden aura, Rodney's cellphone and the folded sheet of paper floated to Bush.

"Ah man," Rodney enthused. "That's what's up."

Bush unfolded the paper and scanned it. "Confidence rate less than sixty percent," he said, wincing at the paper.

"I know, right? Like rolling dice with someone's life."

"You found this in the research facility?"

"That's what I said, ain't it?"

Bush handed the phone to Rodney. "Show me the pictures you mentioned."

Rodney grabbed the phone and thumbed the screen for a few seconds before handing it back to Bush. The gauntlet Bush held the phone with softened into a glove as he looked at the screen. The first photo displayed a man gazing at his metallic hand. Bush swiped and saw another picture with the same man, but the man looked much more sickly. Swiping once more, Bush landed on a photo with CSHP1M3T printed bold and centered.

"Did you tell the cops about this?" Bush asked.

Rodney shook his head. "Nah man. That's evidence. I hafta get it to Tiffany. I heard her earlier—is she still around?" Rodney looked toward the door.

"Tiffany?" Bush asked.

"Yeah, Tiffany Stephens. Yo Tiffany! You out there?"

"The lawyer?"

"Yeah. I heard her voice earlier. Tiffany!"

"I didn't see her."

"Oh."

"I'm going to hold on to these," Bush said, waving the

sheet of paper and phone. "But I'll make sure she gets them." He walked toward the door.

"Where you goin'?" Rodney asked.

Bush stopped at the door and turned to him. "To find your friend. Where does he live?"

Rodney sighed, and after a few seconds, he said, "His grandma's house."

"You know the address?"

Rodney sucked his teeth. "Man, you know I know," he said before sighing again, then telling Bush the address. "Just remember—Tripp isn't a bad dude."

Bush nodded, then exited the room and stepped into the hallway on his way toward the break room.

"Tiffany is the chick we followed last night, right?" Baadaye asked.

"Yep," Bush said.

"I believe she is the woman Tripp Coleman was referring to when he stated *they have her*," Zamani said.

"Me too," Bush said, entering the break room. "We need to find her and Coleman."

"Where should we start?" Baadaye asked.

"Perhaps we should visit Coleman's home since we have the address," Zamani said.

Bush nodded. "Yep, that's my thinking."

"Really?" Baadaye said. "If I was him, I wouldn't go there."

"Maybe," Bush said. "I'm open to a better suggestion."

Baadaye said nothing.

"Okay. We're heading to his house then," Bush said, flying through the broken window and into the sky.

CHAPTER TEN

A FEW BLOCKS away, on the street, Coleman leaned against a building. Unable to maintain his chained form, he ambled along the sidewalk as regular Tripp Coleman. Bystanders looked at him and whispered as they passed by. Coleman wiped the perspiration from his face and rested his back against a wall.

What's going on? he said to himself. *Feeling weak.*

Food aromas wafted through the air. Coleman's stomach growled as he looked and saw a food cart up the sidewalk. While making his way toward the cart, his nose and brain recognized a distinct smell more and more with each step.

"Turkey legs, get your turkey legs," a chubby, bald man behind the cart invited passersby.

Coleman hurried to the cart and snatched a turkey leg from the pan.

"Hey, pal, you plan on paying for that?" the bald vendor asked.

Coleman nodded while chomping down on the turkey leg. The chubby man watched in disbelief as Coleman ate the turkey leg to the bone, then grabbed another leg and started on it.

"Hey," the bald man said, gripping Coleman's hand. "Pay up!"

Coleman stared at the man. "I'll pay you later," he said.

"No, buddy, you'll pay me now!"

Coleman glared at the man. He could feel the chain links crawling across his face, beneath his skin.

The chubby man's eyes widened, and he raised his arms in a surrender posture. "Okay, okay. Ju—just pay me later."

Coleman finished the second turkey leg before clutching some fries and two bananas from the cart on his way toward an alley. He finished the fries and started on a banana before entering the alleyway. By the time he reached the opposite end, he had finished the second banana and stepped onto a sidewalk next to a street occupied by honking and speeding vehicles. Coleman squirmed at the unease from the chain links crawling beneath his skin and throughout his body. He balled his fist and chains enveloped his hand.

"Much better," he uttered to himself while grinning and inspecting his fist. After a moment of quiet reveling, Coleman's brows furrowed. "Tiffany."

A multitude of thoughts raced through his mind. Mainly about Tiffany's safety and how the hero got in the way of him saving her. Then the question of how to find her came front of his mind. Coleman pondered the question before considering an emotionally charged notion he held. He figured he'd go downtown to Sharpe Medical Technologies headquarters, like he had many times before, to see Curtis Sharpe. Except this time, he wouldn't plead for a meeting with Sharpe to discuss the conditions of his sick grandma. No. He'd have his hand around Sharpe's throat, demanding the corrupt businessman give Tiffany back and confess his abuse and negligence. And if he didn't comply, Coleman felt prepared to do whatever necessary to get his own justice.

"This must be the address," Bush said as he descended toward a patchy lawn with nearly a dozen emergency responder vehicles surrounding it.

"What gave it away?" Baadaye asked. "The decorative cop cars scattered around the yard? This is why I didn't think he'd come here."

"Remain positive, Baadaye," Zamani said.

"Yeah, yeah."

Bush landed near the center of the yard, and a bulky officer sporting a buzz cut and full beard immediately approached him.

"Hey. You're that hero, Zambam," he said.

"It's Zambaa," Bush corrected.

The officer threw a dismissive wave. "Yeah, sorry. How can I help you?"

"You're in charge?"

"I am. Officer Dean Fisher," the man said, extending his hand.

Bush shook it. "Nice to meet you, Officer Fisher. Can you fill me in?"

"Sure thing," Fisher said, turning and walking toward the house with Bush behind him. "Officers came to this address to follow up on the break-in at Sharpe's research facility. You know, the one where the explosion—"

"Yep. I know," Bush interrupted as they approached the house's front door.

"Okay. Well, when they arrived, they found the suspect, Tripp Coleman, inside. According to the officers, Mr. Coleman became very aggressive when they asked him to open the door."

"I'm sure they asked nicely."

"What?"

"Ah, nothing," Bush said.

He followed Fisher through the door and caught the attention of every police officer inside as he and Fisher stopped in the living room. Debris and furniture lay scattered across the room. Bush looked at the ceiling and saw exposed wood splintering through a large hole.

Fisher noticed him looking. "As I'm sure you know," he said, "the suspect has some kind of enhanced ability." Fisher looked around the room, then shook his head. "Sent the officers to the hospital."

"Yeah, I've seen his abilities firsthand. Something he acquired at Sharpe's research facility."

Fisher squinted. "Really? How?"

"A chemical. CS—"

"CSHP1M3T," came a voice from near the kitchen.

A slender man with dark slacks and a button-down shirt stepped from behind the counter. The man adjusted his round-framed glasses as he approached Bush and Fisher.

"This is Dr. Steven Conly," Fisher said introducing the man.

Bush nodded. "Dr. Conly, nice to meet you."

Conly's eyes widened and a smile grew on his face. "It's nice to meet you. Wow! Can't believe you're standing here."

"It's not that big of a deal," Bush said.

"For me it is. Fascinating," Conly enthused while scanning Bush over.

Bush glanced at Fisher.

"Dr. Conly is a—a consultant Chicago PD uses for these kinds of... situations," Fisher said.

"Situations?" Bush said.

Fisher shrugged. "Yeah. Ever since you showed up and fought that giant gorilla looking thing, law enforcement has been scrambling to prepare for when we face attacks of that scale." Fisher pointed at Conly. "Dr. Conly is an expert at that sort of thing."

"How do you know about CSHP1M3T?" Bush asked Conly.

Conly sighed. "I worked for Sharpe Medical Technologies," he said.

"Really?"

"Yes. Some time ago."

"Why'd you leave?"

"Let's just say I didn't agree with Curtis' methods."

Fisher chuckled. "Seemed to be more than that," he said. "Heard you two got into a fistfight."

Conly rubbed his hand across his kinky, salt-and-peppered mini afro, then glanced at Fisher. "Not my finest moment, but Curtis Sharpe is a greedy, selfish jerk, and I no longer wanted a part of anything involving him."

"How involved were you with the CSHP1M3T project?" Bush asked.

Conly chuckled. "Very. I'm an expert in biomedical engineering and robotics. It's mostly based on my research, so I practically invented it."

"Dr. Conly's a genius," Fisher chimed in. "You should see what he's cooking up for us at the PD. It's a—"

"It's confidential," Conly interrupted Fisher.

Bush squinted.

Conly shrugged. "The city hired me for a project to equip Chicago's finest with the tools to handle..." He paused, pursed his lips, and glanced at the floor, carefully considering his next words. "Well, to handle extraordinary threats as they emerge," he finished.

Bush had questions concerning these *extraordinary threats* but felt there were more pressing matters, so he responded by simply raising an eyebrow. "Since this chemical is yours—"

"No, it's not mine. Sharpe Medical Technologies owns it. I just discovered how to create it."

"Fair enough," Bush said, hunching his shoulders and shaking his head. "You're very familiar with the technology is what I'm saying. Have you ever seen a situation like Coleman's?"

Conly shook his head. "Never. Somehow, he's able to continuously generate and manipulate the metallurgy at will. I've never seen that in any of the tests. The subjects always only created enough biometallic tissue to replace a limb or heal a wound, but that's it."

"Subjects?"

Conly winced. "Yeah, mice."

"So, there were no human subjects?" Bush asked, his mind going to the picture of the frail man on Rodney's phone.

Conly eyebrows furrowed. "No, not during my tenure, at least. The chemical synthesis wasn't ready for human trials before I left. And judging by this young man's condition, it's still not."

"You mentioned he shouldn't be able to generate more metal. What could make that possible?"

Conly inhaled, then slowly exhaled. "Not sure," he said, shaking his head. "Maybe they modified the synthesis, or a foreign metal was introduced when he came into contact with the chemical." Conly pointed his wagging index finger toward the ceiling. "Yeah, that's a possibility. The foreign metal's biometric marker doesn't match the markers of the trace metals his body naturally produces through ingestion. So, his body continues to produce biometallic tissue, since there's a miscommunication between the foreign metal and the body's trace metals."

Bush glanced at Fisher. Fisher glanced back and hunched his shoulders as if to say he wasn't following.

Conly folded his arms and stared into space. "It'll kill him, unless he's on a diet rich in trace metals, but no human would live long on that kind of diet. Either we force the foreign and trace metals to homogenize, or the chemical needs to be purged from his body." Conly placed a hand over his mouth.

"Can it be done?" Bush asked. "Can we remove the chemical?"

"There's a serum that slowly extracts the synthesis from the body."

"Where is it?"

Conly sighed. "I—I'm not sure where it's at," he said, shrugging. "But I'm certain Curtis Sharpe would know."

Bush nodded at Conly. "Thank you, Dr. Conly," he said before turning to Fisher. "Nice meeting you, Officer Fisher." Bush immediately darted toward the front door.

"Where ya goin?" Fisher called after him.

"To pay Sharpe a visit," Bush said on his way out the door.

"That Dr. Conly is most informative and entertaining," Zamani said as Bush stepped onto the front lawn.

"Yeah, if you're a science dictionary," Baadaye replied. "Do we know where Sharpe is?"

"His company's headquarters is downtown. Let's start there," Bush said before rocketing into the sky.

Tripp Coleman passed a small group of protesters on his way across the street to Sharpe Medical Technologies headquarters. As he walked toward the entrance for the twenty-story structure, people entering and exiting the building stared at him. Coleman ignored the looks and entered through the revolving door, then into a lobby, where more judgmental gazes met him. He remained unfazed. He was on a mission.

"I'm here to see Curtis Sharpe. Is he in?" Coleman asked the girl sitting at the receptionist's desk.

The young lady winced at the sight of him. "Ah… do you have an appointment with him?" she asked, while turning to her computer screen.

"You can say that."

"I don't see anything scheduled for this time today. What did you say your name was?"

"Is he in?"

"Yes, but he's not taking any appointments now."

"He'll hafta squeeze me in," Coleman said before pacing toward the elevators.

"Wait, sir. Security!" the young lady called to a guard standing near a coffee station next to a sitting area by the elevators.

The guard quickly placed his coffee on the station's countertop and raced to the elevators, obstructing Coleman's path. He raised his palm toward Coleman. "Hey buddy, stop there," he said, placing his freehand on the firearm holstered to his hip.

Coleman continued toward the elevators without missing a stride.

"I said stop," the guard asserted while removing his gun and aiming it at Coleman.

Gasps, shrieks, and footsteps skittering echoed throughout the lobby.

Coleman stopped, leaving two yards of distance between him and the guard. "Curtis Sharpe," he said. "What floor is he on?"

"What? Put your hands in the air now."

Chains swaddled Coleman's body. The guard flinched at the sight, then steadied his aim. But before he could pull the trigger, Coleman slung a chain and knocked the gun from his hands. Another chain wrapped around the man's neck. The guard clenched the chain around his throat as his feet left the floor and his back slammed against a wall.

"I'll ask one more time," Coleman said. "Curtis Sharpe, where is he?"

"Ah… sixteen—the sixteenth floor," the guard said struggling to get the words out.

Coleman released the chain, and the guard dropped to the floor while coughing and rubbing his neck. Coleman selected the button for the sixteenth floor and waited seven seconds before deciding the elevator's car was taking too long. He pried the elevator's doors apart and entered the shaft. Noticing the car at the very top, Coleman discharged multiple chains from his body and climbed to the sixteenth floor. He pried opened the floor's shaft doors, then stepped into a wide, bright, empty hallway. A large, walnut-colored hardwood door met him at the end of the hall. As he approached, he noticed the door was open a slit. Coleman nudged the door completely open and entered a secretary's anteroom, but there was no secretary at the desk. He approached a door next to the desk, and as he did, he heard voices shouting on the opposite side.

"We had to get outta there," a familiar voice said. "He had some type of armor and could throw chains, and then Zambaa showed up too, so—"

"So, you thought it was smart to bring her here, to my office," another distinct but familiar voice interrupted.

"They have her," Coleman growled to himself. He twisted the doorknob and discovered that it was locked.

Coleman aimed his palms at the door. A barrage of chains lashed from his arms and ripped the door into pieces. Using his shoulder, Coleman forcefully crashed through the door's remnants. Four pairs of eyes with four accompanying gaping mouths fixed on him as he entered a large office. Dressed in a suit and tie, Sharpe sat at an executive desk that made him look much smaller than he was. Behind him, a triple casement window framed Chicago's skyline. Opposite the desk stood the muscular bald man, the pale man who called himself Agent Beckett, and one of the men in tactical gear who tailed them at the hospital.

Sharpe jumped from his chair while the other three men aimed their guns at Coleman.

"Where is she? Tell me," Coleman demanded, hurrying across the marble floor toward the group.

"Handle it," Sharpe instructed his men before darting toward a seven-foot shelf to his right.

Multiple ear-rocking blast stuffed the area as the three men fired their pistols. Coleman swung his forearm in front of himself, and a chain bundle spiraled into a large circle. The bullets ricochet off the circular shield, then clinked to the floor.

"This is useless," Beckett said.

Coleman lowered his arm, and the shield unraveled, the chains retracting into his forearm as he continued toward the men. "I asked a question!"

Sharpe removed a tubular object from a small chest sitting on one of the middle shelves. "Get the pulse shocker," he told the bald man.

The muscular man darted to a door on his left while Beckett and the tactical-outfitted man fumbled in a rush to reload their guns. They changed their pistol magazines, but before they could aim their guns, Coleman lashed two chains at the men. The chains restrained the men's arms to their sides, and Coleman slung them. Their guns fell to the floor, and the two men hollered as they soared through the air, then crashed into the shelf, barely missing Sharpe as he ducked out of their path. Sharpe crawled behind his desk. Coleman stepped over the two unconscious men and the broken debris from the shelf and followed Sharpe to the desk.

Kneeling with both hands also on the floor, Sharpe looked at Coleman's boots, then slowly lifted his gaze to his chain-swathed face.

"On all fours, just like a dog," Coleman snarled as a chain spiraled from his arm and wrapped around Sharpe's neck, heaving the corrupt businessman from the floor to eye level. "Where is she?"

"Down… downstairs," Sharpe said struggling to speak.

"Where downstairs?"

Before Sharpe could answer, a door smacked against the

wall and the bald, muscular man stood on the opposite side of the doorway. There was something different about him. He wore a metallic jet pack covered by a white, fiberglass casing, with red stripes running along its edges. Flexitubes ran from the jet pack and connected to oval disks attached to his gloved hands.

The bald man aimed his palms at Coleman, and a sonic blast emitted from his hand. A beam of energy engulfed Coleman. The chain-wrapped man dropped to one knee and slung Sharpe to the floor. Coleman gritted his teeth as the chains around his body slowly unraveled. Straining under the blast, he mustered enough strength to clench Sharpe's desk chair with his chains and sling the chair at the bald man. The man dove to the floor, out of the speeding chair's trajectory, allowing the chair to take a chuck out of the wall behind him.

Coleman stood. He felt a pinch in his back as the chains swathed the unchained portions of his body. Sharpe stood behind him with a syringe in his hand.

"What was that?" Coleman barked, walking toward the unscrupulous man.

Sharpe's eyes widened as he stepped back. He glanced at the syringe in his hand and his lips moved, but nothing came out.

As Coleman reached for the scrawny man, he felt a shock hit his side, then he heard glass shatter, and before he knew it, he was falling from the sixteenth floor. The wind whistled as he plummeted toward the parking lot below. He slung a chain and gripped the ledge on the ninth floor. The effort broke his fall long enough for him to swing to the sixth floor's ledge and grip a window jamb while he regained his composure. But he had little time. The muscular, bald guy soared from the broken window. Coleman quickly spawned a shield as the man directed a sonic blast at him.

The blast struck Coleman's shield and knocked the chain-wielding man from the ledge. Coleman once again descended toward the parking lot. As the pavement drew closer, he crossed his arms in a self-hugging posture. Chains immediately discharged from his arms and chest, then spun into a metallic sphere, enclosing him. The metal sphere crashed into the concrete. The chains around Coleman untangled, and a horn blared as a swerving car nearly hit him on its way out of the parking lot. Coleman crawled to his knees inside the enormous crater his fall created and watched as the bald man hovered toward him with his jet pack engine howling.

The bald man aimed his palms at Coleman. "Stay down!" he shouted over his roaring jet pack engine.

"Like that's gonna happen," Coleman said under his breath.

He jumped to his feet and threw a grapefruit-sized, chained-ball while diving from the hovering man's sonic wave counterattack. The blast deepened the crater in the parking lot, and the jet pack wearing man dodged the chained ball hurled at him. Coleman slung a chain and caught the bald man's legs. He gave the chain a hard tug and the floating man crashed to the pavement.

Coleman walked toward the bald man sprawled next to the crater. "Now you stay down," he said, towering over the bald man with his fist raised.

As Coleman prepared to deliver a finishing blow to the man, three loud booms echoed across the parking lot, followed by three speeding objects ricocheting off his back. Coleman turned to find a man in tactical gear standing next to a black cargo van, pointing a pistol at him. He remembered the man from the hospital. As Coleman stepped in the man's direction, a shock struck his back, and he toppled across the pavement.

"Get her out of here," the bald man yelled to the man in tactical gear.

"Her?" Coleman said, slightly out of breath as he crawled to his feet.

The man in tactical gear hurried into the cargo van and brought the engine to life. Coleman raced toward the van, but the bald man intercepted him with a flying tackle. They soared from the parking lot and landed on the street. Exhaust fumes coated the road. The two men stood and squared off. Cars honked and evaded them while passersby gasped and scurried away from the scene.

"I'm gonna end you," Coleman growled.

The van's tires screeched as the vehicle made a hard left turn onto the street.

"Tiffany," Coleman said, watching as the van kicked up dust.

The bald man hit the distracted, chain-shrouded man with a sonic blast. Coleman crashed into a car parked at the curb. The car alarm blared as glass dispersed all over him, the car, and the street. The bald man jetted to the van and landed on its roof. Coleman pushed himself away from the mangled car and gave chase.

CHAPTER ELEVEN

"WHERE'S THIS BUILDING?" Baadaye asked as Bush sailed twenty-stories above downtown.

"Relax," Bush said. "It's just up the street. Are you feeling ok—"

"Oh my," Zamani interrupted.

"What?" Bush looked below and saw a black cargo van swerving in and out of traffic. "Something's going down," he said, swooping toward the street, following the erratically maneuvering vehicle.

As he closed the distance between himself and the van, he noticed a bald man standing on its sunroof.

"Is that a jet pack?"

Sparks trailed the van. Bush noticed a chain attached to the vehicle's back bumper and followed it back to Tripp Chain, who he now knew as Tripp Coleman. The van pulled Coleman along and the chain-shrouded man surfed the streets like a barefoot skier.

Bush stopped and hovered above, assessing the situation. "Well, I think I know why he's after the van," he said.

"Indeed," Zamani said. "We must proceed with caution."

Bush dove toward the van's roof. The man with the jet

pack raised his oval-shaped, gloved hand at the soaring hero and an energy wave pulsed toward Bush.

"Whoa," Bush exclaimed, dodging the blast and watching as its energy stream dissipated into the sky's expanse.

"Wow. You don't see that every day," Baadaye commented.

Bush darted toward the van while hitting the jet pack wearing man with an energy blast, knocking the bald man to his butt and sliding him toward the front of the vehicle. The man crawled to his feet, and Bush readied himself. The two squared off as if they were preparing for an old fashion quick draw. Bush moved first but immediately felt cold metal wrap around his shoulders. Coleman jumped onto the van's roof and landed behind him.

"What are you doing?" Bush asked.

The jet pack man lifted his hand to deliver a blast. He knew the attack would hit both Bush and Coleman, so a grin arched on his face. Coleman's mouth slightly gaped, and he froze. Bush fidgeted under the chain's restraints and flicked his palm toward the bald guy. A golden orb encircled the man's hand as he released another sonic blast. The orb contained the blast, causing the energy to implode and fling the jet pack wearing man from the van. The van immediately weaved out of control. When the debris cleared, Bush saw a hole in the van's roof's main cabin. The driver lay hunched over the steering wheel, unconscious.

Bush struggled under the chains. "We don't have time for this, Coleman," he said.

Coleman slung Bush toward the sky and walked toward the front of the vehicle. Bush spiraled in the air briefly, before orienting himself and darting after the van. Coleman staggered toward the hole in the van's roof. Halfway there, he dropped to one knee and palmed the side of his head. The chains covering him slowly unraveled.

"He must've overexerted himself again," Bush said on his way to the van.

When he was ten feet away from the roof, the van swerved and scraped three cars lined at the curb, taking side mirrors and paint with it as the erratic vehicle continued weaving up the road. Bush looked down the sparsely occupied street and saw a large orange sign warning about construction ahead. Two blocks away, a cement truck with construction cones and workers in reflective vest surrounding it sat parked in the van's path.

"We gotta get this thing in the air now," Bush told Zamani and Baadaye as he aimed the gauntlets at the van.

Golden energy projected from the gauntlets and huge, holographic looking replicas of the gauntlets scooped the van in their palms. Bush kept his hands cupped, lifting them toward the sky. The construction workers hollered, fussed, and scrambled as the van approached and barely cleared the cement truck's mixing tank. Bush continued to hoist the van higher.

"Marvelous save, Calvin," Zamani said.

"If I had a heart, it would've had an attack," Baadaye said.

"This feels awfully familiar."

"It does. Probably because we did something similar with a van yesterday."

"That's it."

"Geez, I thought you were the one who sees the past, Zamani."

"You guys are right," Bush said. "This is the same type of van."

Bush flew the revving vehicle a few more blocks to the coastline before settling it on an empty plot of sand near the beach. The van's tires spun, but the vehicle didn't move. It just dug itself deeper into the sand. Over the crashing waves and squawking seagulls, sirens cried in the distance. Bush zipped to the driver's side, pushed the gearshift to park, turned off the vehicle, then checked the man at the wheel. The tactical-outfitted man gasped labored breaths, but he didn't appear to have any major injuries. Bush sat him upright, resting his back against the seat. On the roof, Coleman lay in his regular form. Bush encircled him in an energy bubble, then placed him on the sand.

Turning his attention to the back of the van, Bush aimed his palms at the doors, then separated his hands a few inches. The van's back doors flung open. Tiffany Stephens lay on the floor, her arms tied behind her back with duct tape. Her legs were also tied. When she noticed Bush, Zambaa to her, Tiffany groaned behind the strip of tape covering her mouth. Her hair frizzed across the floor and in front of her face, partly covering the mascara running from her eyes. Bush removed the duct tape from her legs, arms, and mouth.

"Ms. Stephens?" he asked.

She stared at him but said nothing.

"Are you okay?" Bush continued.

She nodded.

"Okay, let me help you out."

As Bush exited the van with Tiffany, multiple cop cars approached the coastline.

"Tiffany!" Coleman said over the wailing sirens.

"Oh no," Baadaye said. "It's about to happen."

"What is about to happen?" Zamani asked. "Baadaye, did you receive a glimpse?"

Baadaye didn't answer.

"Tiffany!" Coleman called again.

Tiffany circled the van, and Bush followed her. Coleman sat kneeling in the sand, fixed on Tiffany and Bush.

"Tripp!" Tiffany called.

She started toward him, but seeing the officers approach the area with their guns aimed, Bush stopped her.

"Let her go," Coleman said, nearly out of breath.

"We have to help him," Tiffany said.

"I will," Bush assured her.

Coleman attempted to stand. "Let her go or I'll rip you apart," he said before falling to the sand.

"She's safe," Bush said. "You've overexerted yourself. Reserve your energy."

Coleman raised his fist and strained, but nothing happened. He shifted to a kneeling position and looked at his palms. "What's happening? I lost it." He stared into space momentarily. "That needle… Sharpe!"

"Needle?" Bush said.

"Oh boy," Baadaye said.

A chubby officer with a bandage wrapped around his head approached. "Freeze! No one move!" the officer asserted as five more cops joined him and surrounded Coleman.

Bush led Tiffany behind the van and away from the activity before stepping toward Coleman.

"I can't watch this," Baadaye said.

"Lower your weapons," Bush instructed the officers. "This man has lost his enhanced abilities and is a victim of malpractice."

"No. Because of him, my friends are lying in a hospital bed," the chubby man responded.

"He's unarmed. No longer a threat."

"Easy for you to say. How do we know he doesn't have a gun?"

"No, no," Baadaye said.

The hairs on Bush's arms and neck stood up. Despite all his powers and abilities, hearing a policeman utter those words still sent chills through his body. He quickly threw his palms in Coleman's direction and closed his eyes.

"A gun!" the chubby cop shouted.

The police officers opened fire.

"No!" Tiffany's voice screeched over the gunfire's thunderous booms.

The shooting ceased. When Bush opened his eyes, he

stood next to Coleman, inside a golden orb of energy. Outside the orb, bullets lay in the sand surrounding them. Bush felt his muscles tense. A flame ignited in his gut as he glared at the chubby officer.

"I'm only gonna say this once," he said in a calm but eerie tone. "If something happens to him or anyone close to him, I'm gonna hold each of you responsible. Now drop your guns!"

On Bush's last sentence, a golden light erupted around him and illuminated the sky. The police officers immediately dropped their guns. After a moment, the golden aura dissipated and Tiffany ran to Coleman, kneeled, then hugged him.

Baadaye scoffed. "I—I don't see it," he said. "So, it won't happen. Nice!"

"Later, you and I will discuss this further, Baadaye," Zamani said.

Two more squad cars approached the beach.

The chubby officer walked to Bush. "Ah… sorry about that," he said. "But we still hafta take him in."

Bush rolled his eyes, then placed his attention on the cars behind the officer. From one vehicle, Officer Fisher exited from behind the wheel and Conly from the passenger side.

"I see just the man for the job," Bush said.

"Heard all the chatter on the radio," Fisher said as he approached with Conly behind him.

"Officer Fisher," Bush said. "Can you handle taking Mr. Coleman into custody?"

"Sure. But looks like he'll need a medic first." Fisher pointed at Coleman.

Coleman lay sprawled in the sand with Tiffany craned over him, caressing his head.

"Oh my. Medic," Conly called on his way to Coleman.

Tiffany stepped back while Conly examined the exhausted man. Conly checked Coleman's eyes and pulse before waving the paramedics over. They heaved Coleman onto a stretcher and carried him to the back of an ambulance. Bush, Tiffany, Fisher, and Conly all followed.

Coleman looked at Bush as the paramedics opened the ambulance doors. "Hey," he said in a soft tone, almost a whisper. "I guess there's more to you than just spandex."

Bush smiled, then patted his shoulder. "Save your strength."

The medics loaded Coleman into the back. Tiffany jumped in with them.

"Oh, Ms. Stephens," Bush said.

Tiffany turned to him.

From the band around his waist, Bush removed the sheet of paper and phone he received from Rodney. "This may help your case," he continued, handing the items to her.

"What is it?" she asked.

"From Rodney."

"Oh, right. Thank you."

A minute later, the doors closed, and the ambulance pulled off.

Conly shrugged. "He seems okay, but I'll head to the hospital and follow up with him. Didn't see any signs of his ability."

"Yeah, it's like they just went away," Bush said.

"Probably a case of overexertion."

Bush shook his head. "This was different," he said. "He mentioned something about a needle."

"The serum."

"Yeah, probably," Bush said before turning to Fisher. "Keep an eye on him. Some of your colleagues have itchy trigger fingers."

"Sure thing," Fisher said. "We'll head there now."

Fisher and Conly disappeared into the crowd of emergency responders. Bush strolled away from the busyness.

"Great work guys," Baadaye said. "Today is shaping up to be a wonderful one."

"You have some explaining to do," Bush said.

"Indeed," Zamani followed up.

"Why didn't you tell us you had a future glimpse?" Bush continued.

Baadaye sighed. "I… I really didn't want it to happen. We see enough of it every day, and I thought me sharing would somehow cause it to happen."

"So, what exactly did you see?"

"Just the officers surrounding Coleman and shooting."

"Baadaye," Zamani said. "I must admit, I am a little disappointed, but glad everything worked out."

"Really?"

"Definitely," Bush said. "No one was seriously hurt. That's what matters. Plus, we now know why you've been acting so weird."

"You guys are the best."

"But no more secrets like that. You see something, let us know. We're a team."

"Well, if you turn the dial off on the beads, how will I be able to tell you anything, Calvin?"

Bush cleared his throat. "We can discuss that later," he said.

"Uh-huh."

"So, where to now?" Zamani asked. "I believe a celebration is in order."

Bushed glanced at the busted black cargo van. "We have to make one more stop," he said before launching into the sky.

After five minutes of flying, Bush arrived at his destination, a twenty-story building. Floating toward the structure, he immediately spotted the floor he wanted. Hovering through a broken window, Bush entered a spacious office. A large executive desk sat directly in front of him. A fair man in a suit stood near a shelf with his back to the window. Curtis Sharpe. Bush thought he looked bigger than he did on TV.

Sharpe turned to face the window as Bush touched down on the floor and crunched across the broken glass.

"Hey," Sharpe gasped, wide-eyed. "Oh, you."

"Yeah, me," Bush said.

"Did you catch that crazy man who attacked me and my staff? I plan on pressing charges."

"Save it, Sharpe. I know you're responsible for him being that way. Just like I know you're responsible for his grandmother's sickness and death."

Sharpe smirked. "Those are some strong accusations, Mr. Hero," he said. "But you have to prove it."

"I will. Just like I plan to expose all your criminal involvement."

"What criminal involvement?" Sharpe asked with a nervous chuckle.

"Bank robbery, for starters," Bush told him.

"You're trespassing. I think it's time for you to leave."

Bush folded his arms. "Consider this warning a courtesy," he said, hovering backward through the broken window and outside. "I'm watching you."

Sharpe glowered at Bush but said nothing.

"See ya around," Bush said before jetting away.

CHAPTER TWELVE

THREE DAYS LATER, in a high-security prison on an island off Lake Michigan's coast, Coleman sat in the hospital ward, handcuffed to a bed.

"How are you feeling?" Conly asked, while inspecting Coleman with a stethoscope.

"I feel better today, doc," Coleman said.

Conly nodded. "Good." He removed the stethoscope from his ears and allowed it to drape from his neck. "Your blood work showed high levels of a protein found in the CSHP1M3T serum. So, it appears our guess was right. You were injected with the serum." Conly walked to a briefcase sitting on a counter. "Which means your powers are gone," Conly continued as he zipped open the briefcase and placed a notebook inside.

Coleman contorted his lips and shrugged.

Conly noticed and faced him. "You no longer have your powers, correct?" he asked.

"If I did, you think I'd be sitting here?"

Conly stared at Coleman for a long moment, then sighed. "Of course," he said before removing the stethoscope from around his neck and placing it inside the briefcase. "Well, next week the prison's doctor will see you from here on out."

Coleman looked away and scoffed while shaking his head.

"But you know how to get in contact with me if you need anything," Conly continued.

Coleman nodded. "Yeah."

Conly grabbed the briefcase and walked to the restrained man. "Take care of yourself," he said, patting Coleman's shoulder.

Conly strolled to the door, opened it, then gave Coleman a goodbye nod before exiting the room. Coleman sat in silence, alone with his thoughts. Less than ninety seconds later, two armed guards entered the room. One uncuffed Coleman from the bed while the other waited by the door. The guard with the handcuffs instructed Coleman to place his hands behind his back before cuffing them. The three men exited the room and walked through a bright hallway, then turned left at the end of the hall.

"My cell's the other way," Coleman said.

"You have a visitor," one guard told him.

They walked through two security checkpoints before entering the visitor's area. There were ten partitions in the room. Each contained an LED screen with built-in cameras, a corded handset, and a chair. The guard removed Coleman's handcuffs, then pointed to the fourth partition. Coleman glanced at him as he made his way to the chair. A smile arched on his face when he saw who was on the screen. Coleman immediately sat in the chair and grabbed the handset.

"How are you?" Tiffany asked him.

"A lot better now that you're here."

Tiffany dropped her gaze and did her best to conceal her smile. Coleman smiled at her attempt.

"Any word about Rodney?" Coleman asked.

"Yeah. He's out of the hospital, but in police custody. His trial is in a week."

Coleman hung his head. "This is all my fault," he said with a sigh.

"This isn't all your fault."

"I'm in prison and Rodney will probably be too. I just wanna bur—"

"Hey, hey, look at me."

Coleman slowly lifted his head and focused on the screen.

"I'm going to get you out of here, out of this. Rodney too."

"Yeah. Meanwhile Sharpe gets away."

Tiffany shook her head. "No. With the information the group I'm working with gathered, and the evidence you and Rodney found, I believe I have a strong case to present to the district attorney."

"Right."

"He won't get away with what he did."

Coleman folded his arms but said nothing.

"Just promise me you'll keep low and stay away from trouble while I work on getting you out."

"Sure."

Tiffany inhaled, then slowly exhaled. "Can I get you anything?" she asked.

"Just keep an eye on my grandma's house."

"I'll do that. Anything else?"

"Nah. I'm aight."

Tiffany smiled. "Look. I have to go, but I'll be back to see you soon."

"I already can't wait."

"Hang in there. Okay?"

Coleman nodded. The screen went black, then the guard called for him. They cuffed him again, then escorted him to his cell.

"Get comfortable, sunshine," one guard said. "You're gonna be here for a while."

Coleman didn't respond. He just stood and watched as the door closed, then thumped shut. As the guards' footsteps faded in the distance, Coleman balled his fist. Metallic chains swathed around his hand. Inspecting his fist, he smiled. "Whateva you say."

Four hours later, and six miles away, Bush exited his work building. Norman caught up with him and they walked to the bus stop together.

"It was nice to get outta the building and grab lunch today, right?" Norman asked.

"Yeah," Bush said. "I actually had fun. I really needed that."

Norman poked Bush with his elbow. "See. It's good to relax sometimes."

Bush nodded. "Yeah, I guess you're right," he said.

A bus pulled up and stopped at the curb.

"Whatta you got planned for later?"

"I hafta right a wrong from last week."

"So, you have a date," Norman said as the bus doors hissed open.

"Did I say that?"

Norman rolled his eyes. "Tell Lisa hi for me," he said on his way to the bus.

"How did you two become friends?" Baadaye said. "It's just a strange combination."

"I often wonder the same," Zamani said.

"Can't be anymore stranger than my friendship with you two," Bush said.

Bush walked for fifteen minutes with Zamani and Baadaye talking in his head. Usually after five minutes, he would've told them to be quiet or have turned the dials off, but this time he allowed the mostly random conversations to go on. He found himself quietly chuckling most of the time. Bush entered Lincoln Park and located a spot in the grass where trees canopied above, providing plenty of shade. He shrugged off his backpack and removed a blanket, which he opened and laid over the grass. Reaching back into the backpack, he removed a small container with sandwiches, fruit, grape juice, and two plastic cups inside.

"I believe Ms. Lisa will enjoy this," Zamani said.

"He better hope so," Baadaye commented, causing the group to chuckle.

Bush sat, listening to the birds chirp above, the squirrels rustle the leaves and foliage below, and the shouts of excitement from multiple individuals playing throughout the park. Shortly after, he saw Lisa making her way up the trail. Bush stood and waved her over. She walked to him and surveyed the area.

"What's this?" she asked, shrugging and biting her lip in an attempt to mask her surprise.

"First," Bush said. "Thank you for coming." He pointed at his picnic area. "And this is to say I'm sorry for our last date."

Lisa folded her arms, then sighed and looked away.

"C'mon, Lisa. I'm trying."

"I just don't get you," she said, facing him. "My coworker called, checking on me because of the explosion. You said you had to go to the restroom. By the time I finished talking to her, you were gone. And never came back."

Bush sighed.

"It's not the first time you've done that, Cal."

He nodded. "I know."

"Why? Why have you been—distant?"

Bush glanced at the ground. "I... I... can't—"

"Is this about what happened that day at work? The crazy wizard guy and Zambaa?"

Bush nodded. "Yeah, actually it is."

"Are you talking to anyone about it? I am."

Bush shrugged as if to say it's not that simple.

Lisa stepped to Bush and grabbed his hand. "Why didn't you tell me you were struggling with that?"

"Well, I wouldn't say it's a struggle as much as it just changed my life."

"You know you can always talk to me about it."

"I know. But sometimes it feels too complicated to explain, you know?"

Lisa stared at Bush but said nothing. Just pursed her lips and continued to hold his hand.

"So, what do you have here?" she said, walking to the picnic area.

"I made sandwiches," Bush said as they sat on the blanket.

"You're so sweet," Lisa said, leaning back on her arms and watching as a family tossed and chased a Frisbee across an open, grassy field. She took in a breath. "This is a lovely day," she said on her exhale.

"It's beautiful," Bush said as they fixed on each other's faces.

"Get it, C.B.," said Baadaye's voice entering Bush's head.

"Shh. They're going to kiss," Zamani's voice said.

Bush and Lisa kissed, then locked eyes.

"Do it again, C.B.," Baadaye said.

Bush smiled.

Lisa returned the smile. "What?" she asked.

Bush shook his head and turned the dials on his beaded bracelets off. "Nothing," he said. "Just this is a moment when I don't wanna be in my head."

Bush held Lisa, and they kissed again.

THANK YOU FOR READING

I have a favor to ask. If you have a moment, I would really appreciate it if you could leave a short review on the page where you purchased this book. I'm thankful for you sharing your feedback about this book. It really helps new readers find this series.

Sign up for notifications of new books by Alex Cage and exclusive giveaways

www.AlexCage.com/signup

ALSO BY ALEX CAGE

More action thrillers by Alex Cage. Have you read them all? Grab your next adventure today!

Zambaa Superhero Series

Zambaa: Mask and Gauntlets

Zambaa: Unchained

Orlando Black Series

Carolina Dance

Bayside Boom

Bet on Black

Leroy Silver Series

Contracts & Bullets

Aloha & Bullets

Politics Thieves & Bullets

Get the latest releases and exclusive giveaways, sign up to the Alex Cage Reader List.

www.AlexCage.com/signup

JOIN THE READER'S LIST

Get the latest releases and exclusive giveaways - sign up to the Alex Cage Reader List:

www.AlexCage.com/signup

ABOUT THE AUTHOR

Alex Cage is a thriller author and passionate wordsmith who loves to blend his fascination with martial arts and travel with high-octane action and explosive adventures. He enjoys nothing more than entertaining his readers with death-defying missions, larger-than-life characters, and suspenseful stories that always find a way to keep you on your toes.

As the author of nearly a dozen titles, including the Orlando Black series and the Leroy Silver series, Alex combines his obsession for thrillers with a sprinkling of fantasy and sci-fi, so that readers will always find something to capture their imagination. He currently resides in North Carolina. When not writing his next novel, you can find him reading and practicing martial arts.

Find out more about Alex Cage (and get a free read):

www.alexcage.com
connect@alexcage.com

ALEX CAGE
CLEAN FAST-PACED ACTION THRILLERS